A CUCKOLD BEGINS

ROB MATTHEWS

fanny press

Kenmore, WA

fanny press

For more information visit www.fannypress.com

A Cuckold Begins
Copyright © 2025 by Rob Matthews

Library of Congress Control Number: 2025937026

ISBN: 978-1-684922-60-4 (Trade Paper)
ISBN: 978-1-684922-61-1 (eBook)

ACKNOWLEDGMENTS

MY THANKS TO PHIL GARRETT for his ongoing support and encouragement.

ONE

PETER

I WAS SIXTEEN WHEN I FIRST MET Sophie. It was at a house party. That might make you imagine loud music and rooms full of sweaty young people getting drunk on cheap beer. Alas, it wasn't that sort of party. A couple of my parents' friends were celebrating their anniversary by having some people round for the afternoon. I'd been to their house many times during my childhood. It wasn't a huge place, but they'd recently had an extension built on to the back and now had a glass-walled room overlooking the garden. They'd pushed the furniture to the side of this room and twenty people could stand up without crowding. I'd reached that awkward transitional stage of sometimes going to places with my parents, sometimes not. I regretted going to this one. I was past the age where my parents' friends acted astonished at how much I'd grown, but I wasn't yet old enough to join in their discussions about the price of gas or which politician was the most crooked. All the kids I'd grown up with had enough sense to get out of gatherings like this, so there was no one my own age there. Smiling and nodding at no one in particular, I drank a glass of Coke then slipped out. I knew where the TV room was and resigned myself to watching something until my folks were ready to go.

Walking along the corridor, I heard the TV. I hoped it had been left on accidentally. The chances were slim of anyone at this party wanting to watch the same programs as me. The door was ajar and I pushed it open.

Sophie was slumped so far down in the sofa she was almost horizontal. Short and thin, she had long black hair, caramel-colored skin, brown eyes, a prominent nose with long, deep nostrils, and glasses with thick black frames. She was dressed in a forest green t-shirt and gray sweatpants. She'd taken off her black cardigan and was using it as a comforter. Her hair was brushed into bangs to try and hide the couple of spots on her forehead. Short of wearing a face mask, she couldn't do much about the ones on her chin. I casually brushed my hair back with my fingers. I wanted her to see my own spots and realize how much we had in common. I had a slight feeling of hope as I saw her. Maybe I'd met a girl who wasn't out of my league. As I came in, she looked up and regarded me with neither pleasure nor concern. "You found an escape pod?" she asked. "I thought I'd taken the last one."

"I took advantage of the natural cover."

I looked at the TV and recognized an episode of *Buffy the Vampire Slayer*. "We can watch something else if you want," said Sophie. "I've seen this one a hundred times."

"So have I, but it's season three, which is the best."

She looked at me sharply. "Season five is the best. I will fight you on this one."

With her skinny arms and legs, she didn't look like a fighter, but neither did I. Wrestling with her would have been a lot of fun, but I settled for saying, "Can we agree they're both great?"

"I'll allow it in the spirit of compromise," she said, before muttering, "I still know I'm right."

I sat next to her, being careful not to let any part of my body touch any part of hers, and we watched the show. I knew better than to say anything. We both understood that *Buffy* is sacred and must be appreciated in reverential silence. Even so, I wasn't completely focused on the program. Sophie was wearing a spiced orange perfume. That, combined with a hint of her sweat, stirred up feelings inside me. Back then, my cock stiffened if it came in contact with a towel, water, or a gust of air so it had no chance of staying soft in such close proximity to a real female. I'm sure the heavy fly on jeans is there specifically to hide erections, but I crossed my legs to make sure she didn't see anything.

MARK

I WAS AT WORK. FOR A TEMPORARY job, it wasn't too bad. I wasn't washing dishes or flipping burgers. My clothes stayed dry and didn't smell of grease at the end of the day. The work was just boring—page after page of figures to be entered into a database. I had no idea what the figures were about and I didn't care. I spent seven hours a day with my fingers on a number pad. My manager assured me the speed and accuracy were good enough so the company kept paying me. That was the only thing I positively liked about this job: the way the number in my bank account went up at the same time every week.

Actually, that's not true. There was another thing I enjoyed. Ashley was the team's assistant manager. It was a better job than mine in that she didn't spend her time glued to a desk. She went from one person to another, solving problems and offering tips on how to work more efficiently. She was five foot tall, plumpish, with dyed blonde hair and a permanent grin. If you'd seen her at work, you'd have assumed she was a nice, slightly ditzy girl. I knew a different side of her.

One afternoon, she walked past me. "There's your pen back," she said, putting a blue ballpoint on my desk. She hadn't borrowed my pen, but I knew what this meant. I picked it up and rested it casually against my upper lip in a contemplative pose. Breathing in, I smelled the sweet scent of Ashley's pussy. She had taken the pen into the toilet and rubbed it between her labia. It was a signal we'd agreed between us. I looked to see where she was in the office and caught her eye. I lowered my chin by half an inch once only. She understood. The rest of the day dragged by. It was hard to concentrate on data entry knowing what was going to happen as soon as the clock ticked round to five.

The electronic screen above the bank of desks finally flashed the message 'TIME TO GO HOME!!!' I didn't look at Ashley. Switching off my computer, I took my coat from the back of my chair. "Hey, Mark," said one of my co-workers, "coming for a drink?"

"Not tonight," I replied, yawning a bit too loudly. "Very tired. Have a good time. See you tomorrow."

I didn't go out the main entrance. Making sure I wasn't seen, I went down the back stairs to the parking garage. I didn't have a car so had no reason to be there. I hid behind a concrete pillar like a stalker in a horror movie and waited for the red Nissan to come by. It stopped in front of me and I got in. Ashley and I sat in silence, doing nothing suspicious. If anyone should happen to see us, it was one colleague giving another a ride home. Nothing odd about that. Only when we were safely inside her apartment could we breathe easily . . . well, more easily. There was always the danger her boyfriend would come home and catch us but that was a big part of the fun, especially for her.

I blew my nose even though I didn't have to and dropped the tissue on the living room carpet. Going into the bathroom without permission, I left the toilet seat up and a couple of piss splashes on the linoleum floor. In the bedroom, I found Ashley already naked in bed. I took off my clothes and joined her. There was something we needed to do before anything else could happen. After putting a finger to her lips, she picked up her phone and dialed a number. Holding the phone in her left hand, she curled her right hand around my cock. "Hey, baby," she said into the phone. "How's it going? It's okay if you want to go to the gym tonight." I was glad I never met her boyfriend. He was probably a big guy judging by how much time he spent at the gym. I'm in pretty good shape myself, but I'd prefer not to get into a fight if I can avoid it. My face helps get the ladies and I didn't want that spoiled by a broken nose or a cauliflower ear. "I'm stuck at work," she continued. "Pile of papers on my desk to get through." We were pretty much a paperless office, but he didn't need to know that. "What time do you reckon you'll be home? That's fine. I'll try to be back by then." She moved down the bed until her head was level with my groin. After silently kissing my cock, she said, "I love you, baby." She ended the call, checked twice that it had disconnected, and put the phone down. "I just lied to my boyfriend," she said, with a wicked glint in her eye.

"Yes, you did." I put my hand between her legs and circled her clit with my middle finger. "You're a lying bitch."

"This is the bed he paid for," she said. "You shouldn't be here."

"I'm touching your pussy. Only he should be allowed to do that."

"I'm a bad girlfriend."

"You're a lying, cheating whore." Her clit was getting wetter under my finger. After she'd had enough of the name-calling, she rolled onto her back and pulled me on top of her. She put my cock into her pussy. As I moved inside her, she said, "My boyfriend loves me. You don't love me, do you?"

"No, I don't," I assured her, "but I'm the one fucking you. I've got my big, hard cock up your slutty cunt. It's better than anything you get from your boyfriend."

"It's so much better," she said.

We never kissed on the lips. That was something she saved for her boyfriend. I kissed all the way round her neck. It always drove her crazy. I squeezed her big tits and pulled her nipples hard enough to make her gasp. I decided to do something extra mean. I put my lips on the upper part of her left tit and sucked hard. I didn't leave any teeth marks, but it left a large red mark in an intimate place. She lifted her breast toward her face so she could see it. "You bastard," she said, in a hoarse voice. "What am I going to tell my boyfriend?"

"Tell him you're a skanky ho and you can't keep your pants on," I suggested.

This made her groan with desire. "Fuck me!" was all she could say.

I increased the speed of my thrusts until I knew from her breathing and her face that she was about to cum. I thought about leaving her unsatisfied but decided to be kind. I slowed down and focused on making each thrust as hard as possible. I rammed into Ashley six times before she threw her head back and her cunt tightened around my cock. I paused to let her enjoy the moment before carrying on. Now she'd cum, it was all about me. I pulled out of her and told her to get on her hands and knees. I liked her big, round ass and wanted to look at it as I shot my load into her. Her cunt was so wet, I couldn't stay inside her. I pulled a corner of the under sheet off the bed and wiped her pussy with it. That gave me enough dry traction to finish fucking her. I was tempted to drag my nails across her buttocks or even scratch my name into them, but that would have been going too far. I enjoyed being with Ashley and didn't want our liaisons to end too soon. I parted her cheeks to get a peek at her tight little asshole—somewhere I'd never been. The sight was enough to push me over the edge and I emptied my balls into her unfaithful pussy.

Pulling out of her again, I picked up her boyfriend's pillow. "Please don't," she said. This was something we'd agreed on. She begged me not to be a jerk and then watched me go right ahead and be a jerk. If she genuinely didn't want me to do something, she said, "Jabberwocky." We figured it was a good safe word as it wasn't something we'd normally drop into conversation during sex. I wiped my dick on his pillow, leaving a long smear across it. That was Ashley's kink with me. I left traces of my presence all over the apartment and, after I'd gone, she had to get rid of everything incriminating before her boyfriend came back. She called it the 'deMarkation' of their home. The nerve-racking risk of it excited her. She couldn't relax all evening as she spent time with her boyfriend. There was always the fear she'd missed something. Her boyfriend must have thought he was living with a clean freak: she changed the bedding and washed the bathroom floor so often. At the time, I wondered how she'd explain the red patch on her tit. Her 'deMarkation' didn't extend to that sort of mark. I found out later that she'd told her boyfriend a tale about someone at work leaving the drawer of a filing cabinet open. She hadn't been paying attention and the corner of the drawer caught her square on the boob as she walked past. He'd bought her story and even kissed the spot better. She said lying to him was almost as erotic as the fucking itself. No one who saw the smiley, friendly girl in the office would have believed how kinky she was. Isn't that true of all of us, though? We present a respectable image of ourselves to the world, but we're all deviant perverts behind closed doors.

I discovered early on that I like women who are in a loving relationship with someone else. It's too easy to have sex with someone who's single and the stakes aren't high enough. I like to know a girl's risking something to be with me.

There are a few drawbacks to this lifestyle. I don't expect anyone to have sympathy for me. After all, I get to have no-strings-attached sex with as many women as I want. Generally, life is good, but there is sometimes an awkward moment after I've fucked a woman in front of her man. They make it clear they want me to leave. I've done my bit and now it's time for them to be alone. It feels a bit rude but I guess I can understand it. Something seismic has just happened in their relationship and they need time together to regroup. He still hasn't cum so, for some couples, that's the first order of business. He reclaims his unfaithful partner by fucking her or else she makes him cum with her hand. Either way, it lasts two seconds. Then comes the reassurance. She tells him she doesn't even like me. It's just sex between her and me. Sometimes, she promises never to see me again. This is another thing I don't like about the lifestyle. It doesn't matter how much I'm enjoying my time with a woman. I know it can end at any point, normally because of a guilt trip. A lot of my affairs finish in the first week of January. She makes a new year's resolution to sort her life out. She's going to cut out the fried food, drink more water, and stop doing the dirty on her man. Even if he approves of her cucking him, it's wrong, it's immoral, and it must end. This is disappointing if I've already come up with some new games to play next time we meet, but I shrug it off quickly and move on to the next one. I can't afford to get attached to someone who's already attached to someone else. All that being said, I love this life. New people, new experiences. I know it has to end at some point. This is a young man's game. I don't want to be one of those sad fifty-year-old men with dyed black hair hanging round bars imagining they can still pull girls in their twenties. One day, I'll have to settle down and that'll mean finding someone who's prepared to detach herself from her man and be mine and mine alone. That's years in the future though. For the moment, guys, keep an eye on your wives and girlfriends whenever I'm around.

Two

PETER

I WAS SHY AROUND THE OPPOSITE SEX when I had that first encounter with Sophie at the house party. I hadn't had much success with girls, not recently, anyway. When I was six years old, there was a girl called Leah who lived next door to us. We spent all our time together and she introduced me to everyone as her boyfriend. Our aunts and grandparents said we made an adorable couple. We even went as far as getting engaged. I got a red plastic ring from a bubble-gum machine, which I presented to Leah. We planned our married life in some detail, agreeing that the cleaning lady would do the downstairs rooms of our house on a Tuesday and the upstairs on a Thursday. Sadly, before we could put our plans into effect, her family moved away. We never officially broke off our engagement, so I hope there aren't any breach of promise lawsuits coming my way. When I was six, I had the advantage of being cute, with light brown hair and chubby cheeks. Growing up stretched that out of me. My face became a long, thin oblong with spots and freckles competing for space. I had to wash my hair twice a day to stop it flopping into a greasy helmet. I was tall and thin with only minimal control over my arms and legs. Girls found me resistible. I got used to hearing the words, "No, thank you," at school discos and, "I don't think of you that way," from girls I knew. I spent many a sleepless night wondering if the girls were picking up on some vibe I was putting out. Did they know I was gay even if I didn't? It was a hypothesis worth testing. One of the women's magazines my mother subscribed to came with a free underwear catalogue. When she wasn't looking, I took it up to my room. Most of the pages were devoted to women in various bras, panties, stockings, and camisoles. There were a couple of pages showing men posing in briefs, boxers, and trunks. My first thought was that women had more interesting things to wear than men. Nonetheless, I forced myself to look at the men. To encourage my arousal, I said things under my breath like, "Check out the bulge on this guy. What I wouldn't give to rub my tongue around those pecs." I ogled the men for twenty minutes and felt nothing. It seemed I wasn't gay. This was confirmed when I turned back to the women and was immediately more interested. I spent more than an hour trying to spot hints of nipple peeping through lacy bras. I fancied women, but what good was that if they didn't fancy me back? I resigned myself to living a life of chastity and would have taken holy orders if I'd been the slightest bit religious.

With all that in mind, it was surprising how comfortable I felt, sitting on the sofa next to Sophie. We didn't speak but the silence was companionable. We watched a couple of episodes of *Buffy* until my dad put his head round the door. "This is where you're hiding, is it?" He looked pleased to see me with a girl. "Who's your friend?"

I realized we hadn't gone through the formality of introducing ourselves. Fortunately, she said, "My name's Sophie."

"Oh yes," said my dad, "you're Caroline's niece."

"That's right."

"We're heading home now," my dad told me.

On my way out, I had the presence of mind to tell Sophie, "My name's Peter, by the way."

She gave me a smile which quickened my heart rate and she said, "*Enchantée.*"

It would have been easy enough to say, "Hey, can I have your phone number? Maybe we can hang out and watch more *Buffy* some time." I didn't say that, though. I just left. After I'd arrived home, I casually asked my dad about Caroline and Sophie. He told me Caroline had originally pronounced her name *Caro-leen* and she and her sister Jeanne, Sophie's mother, had come over to this country from the south of France twenty years ago. That explained the bronze tint to Sophie's skin. You'd assume my next move was clear. My dad was clearly acquainted with the family. There'd have been no problem asking him if he had a number for Jeanne or at least for Caroline. I didn't do that, either. I knew there was no point. I'd never have had the nerve to call. In those days, I assumed I always called people at the worst possible time. The other person would be in the bath, having sex, or both, at the exact moment I chose to phone and they would hate me for interrupting them. I much preferred to write to people. I could have asked my dad for Jeanne's address, but I decided not to. I couldn't bear the idea of sending Sophie one of my witty and well-worded letters, only to wait for a reply that never came. I didn't forget her, though. She featured heavily in my fantasies. If things had panned out the way they did in letters to porn mags, Sophie would have announced *Buffy* always made her super-horny. She'd have ripped off her clothes and mine. After an hour of us vigorously making love on the sofa, three of her girlfriends would have arrived and I'd have satisfied all four of them with my proud member. Real life isn't like that unfortunately and I didn't see her again until five years later, when I went to college.

I was studying computer science. It's hard to imagine a geekier subject but we flattered ourselves we were a few rungs up the desirability ladder from the chemists. We may have talked about user experience and collaborative development, but at least we didn't smell of ammonia.

I was given a welcome pack when I arrived, which included my room number and key. After twenty minutes of going up and down the same staircase and walking through a labyrinth of identical white-painted corridors, I found the right place. Opening the door, I was surprised at how much space there was. I walked into a small living room with a sofa, two armchairs, and a low coffee table. Three doors led off from this area. Behind the first was a bathroom with a checkerboard tiled floor, toilet, and shower. The second door opened onto a room with a bed, desk, wash basin, bedside table, and chest of drawers. The third door led to an identical bedroom. Why did I have two bedrooms? One for during the week and the other for Sunday best? Or did the college assume I'd have visitors coming to stay? Then something struck me and I wasn't sure I liked it. This place was designed for two people to share. It meant I was going to have a roommate. I chose the bedroom closest to the bathroom and unpacked my things. As afternoon turned to evening, I felt more hopeful. No one had shown up so maybe whoever was due to be my roommate had dropped out at the last minute. I might still have this suite all to myself. Then I heard a key turning in the lock and a guy walked in. "Hi, I'm Mark," he said.

MARK

I DIDN'T OFFICIALLY BREAK UP WITH ASHLEY when I quit my job to go to college. I couldn't. She was another man's girlfriend, so she wasn't mine to break up with. I knew I'd be hooking up with girls at college, but I figured it would be a good idea to have someone back home. Summer vacations lasted twelve weeks. I'd have gotten a headache with no one to fuck for that length of time. I didn't have much fear Ashley would forget about me or decide to be faithful to her boyfriend. Let me explain why.

I'm six foot two inches tall with short brown hair and deep blue eyes. I've always been the outdoor type. I spent my childhood climbing trees, building shelters, and running away from the owner of the land where I was trespassing. In later years, I discovered sports and spent most of my time playing them. The result of all this is a good body. I don't have the bulging muscles of a steroid-popping bodybuilder, but my arms and chest have a nice thickness to them. My legs are well toned. I eat whatever I want knowing I'll burn it off, so my abs are hard and flat. You're in danger of breaking your hand if you punch me in the stomach so don't try, no matter what I did to your wife or girlfriend. I'm also very good at sex. This isn't me being arrogant. If a tennis player keeps winning tournaments, he knows he's good at the game. With me, it's all the women telling me I'm the best they've ever had. I'm only going on user feedback. I've taken the time to learn the correct use of my fingers, lips, and tongue. Yes, every woman is different but there are certain touches that work with most of them. Most of all, I've learned how to control my cock. A man will often talk about his penis like it's a badly behaved puppy. It jumps up when it's not supposed to, goes to sleep unexpectedly, and sometimes leaves a mess on the floor. My cock, however, takes orders from central command. If I tell it to get hard, it does. If I tell it not to cum, it doesn't. This means I decide whether I satisfy a woman or not. I don't always give her an orgasm, because I want her to know it's under my control. If a woman knows a climax is a privilege which must be earned, she works harder for it.

I've always found it easy to get the girls, but I don't keep them. It's not that I can't. It's just I don't usually want to. I like discovering a woman's body. Does she have any piercings or tattoos? Does she shave or trim? Does she have a posh girl's nipples that would prefer to go unnoticed with the most subtle darkening of shade? Or does she have working-class nipples that are big, red, and demand attention? It's also interesting to find out about her sexual interests and kinks. Does she want to make love or does she need to be fucked? Does she prefer to be called a precious angel or a dirty whore? It's all exciting to begin with, but it soon gets old. After three weeks,

I've seen her body from every angle and she's got no more fantasies or perversions to fess up to. That's when I start looking round for a replacement. This might sound like a shitty way to treat women. My defense, such as it is, has two parts. One, I'm only doing what most guys would do given the chance. Any man who judges me is doing it with more than a little jealousy in his heart. If he persuades one woman to go to bed with him, he sticks to her like a limpet because he might never get another one. I know I can always get another one and that gives me more freedom. Two, I'm always honest with the women. I never make romantic promises. I make it clear I'm not going to be a boyfriend to them. I definitely don't talk about love or marriage. All I can offer them is the best sex of their lives. Is that such a bad thing to give another person?

You may be asking why I saw Ashley on a semi-long-term basis. The answer is I was turned on by her kink. I went round to the place she shared with her boyfriend and I acted like a dick. Sometimes it's nice to have free rein to behave badly. She was living with this guy, so it wasn't some casual fling. He was potentially the love of her life, her future husband, maybe even the father of her children. She risked losing it all because of her desire for me. The stakes were high enough to keep me coming back for more.

I got into college on a soccer scholarship. I was hoping it would get me out of too much studying, because that's never been my thing. I was looking forward to improving my game by work-ing with top coaches. I was also eager to jump into a new pool of women. I had all but exhausted the girls in the little town where I grew up. I'd fucked half of them and the other half hated me for how I'd treated their friends. (That didn't always stop them going to bed with me, though.) I needed a new hunting ground and college would do as well as any.

You might think I was disappointed when I got to my room in college and found I was sharing with some tall, skinny geek. You'd assume I'd prefer to be with a fellow jock so we could sit around discussing sports and girls over a couple of beers. On the contrary,

I was delighted to unlock the door and find Peter waiting for me. I knew he'd worship me on sight. I wouldn't be bullying him, if that's what you're thinking. He'd be so flattered when I was nice to him that he'd do whatever I wanted to keep me as his friend. He'd do all the shopping, cooking, and cleaning. I wouldn't have to ask him to do my essays for me. All I'd have to do was mention I was finding a bit of work difficult and he'd volunteer to take it off my hands. It would be a pleasure for him to feel he was helping. I could borrow money from him any time, knowing he'd never risk asking for it back. Maybe he had a girlfriend. If he did, I *knew* I'd fuck her and he wouldn't complain about it too much. He'd take it as part of the natural order of life. As the alpha male, I had the right to any woman I wanted. He might even talk her into going to bed with me. Not that she'd need much persuading. If any woman had a free choice between me and Peter, it would only ever go one way. Now, you might be saying, "But, Mark, a geeky guy's girlfriend is herself going to be a nerd or a dork. Don't you have standards?" Yes, I do, but I've been with geeky girls before and I confirm they can be great fun. Some of them have a good dose of self-loathing. If so, I pull their hair while fucking them and spit on their tits, and they take it as no more than they deserve. These girls are also the easiest to get rid of when I'm tired of them. They sigh and say, "I knew you were going to leave me sooner or later." Even the ones who aren't down on themselves can be interesting. Geeks spend a lot of evenings in their room alone. Some of this time is spent thinking up fantasies. They lie in bed and dream about what it would be like to swallow cum, be spanked, try anal. They meet someone like me and I'm only too happy to turn fantasy into reality. This makes for a most enjoyable three weeks.

I walked into the college room, said, "Hi, I'm Mark," and held out my hand.

"Peter," said my new roommate, shaking my hand gratefully. I didn't unpack immediately but dumped my bags on my new bed, except for a black plastic bag which I brought back into the sitting area. "I don't know about you, Peter, but I could use a beer." I took two cans out of the bag and threw one to him, only a little too hard. He didn't catch it of course, but I wasn't going to make a big deal of it. We sat down and talked. I was surprised to find I liked the guy. The little town where he grew up didn't sound so different from mine. His tales of it were funny. I discovered he didn't have a girlfriend, which was disappointing, but not a deal breaker. If I had nothing else to do in the evening, I could imagine worse things than letting Peter make my dinner and having a chat with him.

Looking around, I asked him, "What are we going to call this place?"

He frowned. "Why can't we just call it the room?"

"That won't work. If I text to warn you I'm in the room with a girl, you need to know if I mean my bedroom or this part."

"You want to have girls in here?"

"Dude, you know what fun you can have with a couple of girls, an armchair, and a coffee table?"

"Of course I know," he said, in a voice that made it clear he didn't. "Why don't we call the whole place our pad?"

"A bit hippie, but okay."

"We can call this area the den. Then there's my room and your room."

"That should cut out any confusion."

"If you say you've got a girl in the den, I'll keep out of your way for half an hour."

I grinned. "An hour. Please."

"If you say you've got a girl in the room, I can come back, no problem. You're not likely to have a girl in *my* room."

"Don't rule it out."

Peter rolled his eyes and checked the time on his phone. "Are you coming to the mixer?"

I didn't want the first sight people had of me to be as part of a double act with Peter. "You go. I'll be along later."

He spread his hands. "I can wait."

"No, you can't," I told him urgently. "It's the *girls* who are waiting for *you*."

"Are you sure? Girls don't normally wait for me."

"It's the whole point of a mixer. This is when you'll meet the girls at their most vulnerable. Away from home for the first time, lonely, confused, looking for someone to take care of them. Why shouldn't one of them find her safe haven in your bed? Don't let it stop you for a second if she says she has a boyfriend back home. In the whole history of the world, not one single relationship has survived one of the couple going off to college. Sure, last night, she had a goodbye dinner with him followed by vanilla sex. She lay in his arms afterwards and promised there would never be anyone else. They made plans for him to visit as soon as she's settled in. Then she gets here and she's assaulted from all sides by the sheer newness of the place. She's in a new town surrounded by hundreds of new people. The law of averages says she's going to find some of them attractive. She has more freedom than she's ever had before. She can stay out until two in the morning and get up at midday if she wants to. Her mom isn't here to give her grief about it. She doesn't have to hide in the bathroom if she fancies a cigarette. She can light up in the middle of the quad. Her horizons are broadening. She hears people talking about going on to study in Paris or Rome. They're considering a job with Microsoft or Goldman Sachs. She starts to think she can aim a bit higher and have a life the folks back home can only dream about. Suddenly, the small-town boy she left behind doesn't fit into her future. He's a nice enough guy. If he keeps working hard, he might teach at the local school or manage the drug store, but she's moved on. She's more interested in the guy who's deciding whether to do a master's at Harvard or get into the fast-track management scheme at IBM. She sends her boy back home a letter saying, 'We're not the same two people who fell in love all those years ago,' which is a gentle way of saying, 'I'm too good for you now.' So get yourself along to the mixer. Be the reason some guy gets his heart broken."

THREE

PETER

I WALKED AWAY FROM THE PAD IN a daze. Mark's words had flooded over me. It was hard to believe he was the same age as me. He'd done so much more living and understood the world so much better. I'd have been happy to spend the evening talking to him or, rather, listening to him, but if the mixer was like he said, I couldn't miss the chance.

It was held in the college dining hall and the room had the rich, savory smell of soup and pasta sauce. An effort had been made for the evening. The tables were stacked against the wall. A politically correct banner saying, 'Welcome to our Freshmen, Freshwomen, and Freshpersons!' was hung from the middle of the ceiling. This was not a keg party. Bottles of wine which didn't look like the cheapest in the store were lined up on a side table. Waitresses in black waistcoats, white shirts, and black bow ties made their way through the room with trays of glasses. It was all a lot classier than I was used to. I was wearing jeans and a shirt. I felt I should have made more of an effort. Uncomfortable, I had the urge to leave, but where would I go? Mark would only forgive me going back to the pad so soon if I'd already scored. I could have wandered around campus for a couple of hours, but something told me if I ran away now, that would become my whole life at college. I took a glass of wine from a passing waitress. "Thank you," I said, thinking it might be the longest conversation I'd have with a woman all evening. I carried my glass to the side of the room and leaned against the wall. I studied the women without too much obvious staring.

For girls who were supposed to be lonely and confused, most of them looked like they had it together. Some had gone full cocktail party in black mermaid dresses with minimalist high heeled shoes. Others were more jazz era in head dress, white beads, and elbow length black gloves. If smoking had been allowed at the mixer, they would have been sporting cigarette holders. Then there were those who refused to dress as the establishment dictated. They were in baggy white t-shirts with skinny fit black jeans and basketball boots. However differently the women were dressed, they had one thing in common. They looked comfortable in this place. Holding their wine glasses with the easy confidence of French film stars, they shared with Mark a quality of worldliness. They were talking and laughing like people who were well used to social situations and knew how to shine in them.

I didn't pay so much attention to the guys, but it was impossible to ignore them completely. Most of them were smart casual in jacket and shirt without a tie. Others were more sporting in polo shirt and chinos. They were chatting to each other as if they'd been friends for years. I seemed to be the only person acting the way a new boy should. Had I misread the date for the start of the semester? Had everyone else been here a couple of months already?

The groups were all circles with no obvious gaps in them. I couldn't see any way of breaking in. I glanced at my phone to see how long I had to stay in order to save face. I'd only been there ten minutes. I looked up and scanned the room again. That's when I saw her. She was more elegantly dressed this time. In a red jacket and skirt combo with a long sleeved white top underneath, she looked more like she was at a job interview than a party. She was hovering on the outskirts of one of the groups, not joining in the conversation, but sipping nervously at her drink. I loved that there was someone else in the room who didn't know exactly what to do. The spots had cleared up so she had her dark hair swept back from her forehead. The thick framed glasses were the same. Her gawky figure hadn't filled out. She still had the look of someone who might not be out of my league. Newly emboldened, I strode through the crowd and touched her shoulder. I was on the point of saying, "Remember me?" but decided it would display more manly confidence if I assumed no one who had met me could ever forget me. "Hey, Sophie," I said, nonchalantly, like she was the hundredth woman I'd spoken to. "Long time, no see. How have you been?"

Her mouth opened and her eyebrows went up half an inch. "Peter!" My heart soared. She did indeed remember me. "What are you doing here?"

It was a silly question, but I didn't pick her up on it. "I arrived today. I had a few options, but something told me this was the place to come. Maybe because of the people I meet here." I was doing my best to channel Mark and flattered myself this was sounding pretty smooth.

"What are you studying?" she asked.

I thought about lying and tried to work out what the most glamorous subject was. I figured she'd find out the truth soon enough. "Computer science."

"No way," she said. "Snap."

This was looking better and better. We'd be doing a lot of the same courses. It was like being back at school and having a friend to sit next to in class. "Listen," I said, looking round the room with a bored eye. "This is a bit lame. I saw a sporty-looking Italian place down the road. What do you say we ditch these guys and grab a bite to eat?"

"That would be nice," she said, making my heart soar a whole lot more. "But, Peter, drop the act. Be yourself."

"I'm not sure that's a good idea. Myself isn't all that great."

"I'll be the judge of that."

We slipped out of the mixer without anyone else noticing. As we walked down the road in silence, I worried we wouldn't have anything to talk about. After all, the only thing I knew we had in a common was we'd both liked *Buffy* back in the day. After we were sat at our table, Sophie showed she had her own special way of keeping the conversation going. "You're on death row," she began. "You're going to be executed in the morning." I was taken aback. I've no objection to gothic flights of fancy, but this was a heavy thing to talk about over pizza. "You can watch one movie tonight. What do you choose?" We talked for more than an hour about what we would watch, read, and listen to if we only had one night left on earth. We shared a taste for epic fantasy films and doom-laden music sung by guys in leather trousers with dyed black hair. The questions got a little more personal and it felt increasingly like a first date. "Do you drink much?" she asked.

I still had most of the money my parents had given me at the start of the semester, so I'd tried impressing Sophie by ordering a bottle of the cheapest wine. I held up my glass. "Never touch the stuff," I assured her. "Total abstinence at all times." She smiled. "Seriously, though," I continued. "The occasional glass of wine with dinner or a can of beer at a barbecue. Otherwise, I prefer tea. I'm boring."

That would have been a good moment for her to disagree, but she said, "I'm just as bad. I'd rather have a cup of tea or a can of Coke. Your turn."

"Do you smoke?" I asked her.

She'd have liked to hold up a cigarette and respond in her turn with, "Never touch the things." As it was, she said, "Hardly ever. If I got stressed at work and someone suggested going for a smoke, I occasionally said yes. Why? Are you anti-smoking?"

"It has bad associations for me. One of my teachers at school was a heavy smoker and had a bad case of ashtray mouth. When she was yelling at me for something, it was wave after wave of cigarette breath coming my way."

Sophie looked at me slyly. "She was still beautiful, though."

"What makes you say that?"

"In amongst your expressions of horror and disgust, there were a few nostalgic little smiles."

I blushed. "Well, yes. She was beautiful."

"Part of you looked forward to her chewing you out."

"Maybe a tiny little bit of me," I admitted.

It was after ten when we went back to the campus. I walked her to the block where her room was—only two hundred yards from mine—and we said, "Goodnight, see you soon." I gave her a quick hug, partly because I wanted Mark to smell a woman's perfume on me when I returned to the pad. He'd gone out by the time I got back, having made a couple of important changes to the den. A large television now had pride of place in front of the two armchairs. Beside the larger of the two chairs was a fridge. I had a look inside and wasn't surprised to find no food, just twenty cans of beer. I didn't feel I could take one of Mark's beers without asking. I wasn't even sure I was allowed to watch his TV. It was a good idea to have an early night. The serious business of college began the next day. It was hard to sleep, though. Sophie's face kept flashing into my mind.

FOUR

MARK

A SHLEY WASN'T THE FIRST ATTACHED WOMAN I'd been with. A couple of years before, I'd had a very different experience. I was working in a local bar, even though I was barely old enough to drink myself. Several times, I had the exchange with a customer, "Can I see some ID?"

"I'll show you mine if you show me yours."

It didn't pay well and, for some reason I never understood, people don't tip barmen as often as they do waiters. Even so, I liked the job. It was the sort of place where couples came in for a bottle of beer and a glass of wine so I didn't have to learn any complex mixology. There was a nice bunch of people behind the bar and some cheeky back and forth with the customers. One couple, in particular, made an effort to get to know me. His name was Ray. He was a plump man in his late forties with white hair and the pink face of someone who enjoys the high life. His wife, Angie, was a slim, attractive woman in her early thirties with long, auburn hair and blue-gray eyes. Despite the age difference, I never got a creepy vibe from them. The way they talked to each other always suggested equal partners.

It was clear Angie was into me—nothing unusual about that; she's only human, after all. What struck me as strange was the way Ray encouraged her. One evening, Angie asked me, "New shirt, Mark? It suits you well."

Ray added, "He looks hot in it, doesn't he, Ang?" It was an odd thing for one straight man to say about another.

Another time, I asked her if she'd like her usual large glass of white wine. She replied, "At least someone round here gives me a large one. I only get a small one at home." Far from being annoyed at this dig, Ray laughed as if it was the funniest thing he'd heard in a while.

One evening, Ray beckoned me into a dark corner of the bar and said, "Angie's a fine looking lady, isn't she?"

"She sure is. You're a lucky guy, Ray."

"Well, Mark, she likes you a lot and would like to get to know you better. When you finish up tonight, why don't you come back to our place for a nightcap?"

I still didn't see this as necessarily sexual. What can I tell you? I was young and naïve in those days. Ray and Angie stayed at their table after the bar had closed. When John, my manager, politely suggested they move toward the door, they said, "We're waiting for Mark," which caused John to raise an eyebrow in my direction. After we'd washed all the glasses, wiped the tables, and swept the floor, I picked up Ray and Angie. We walked out together and went to their car. I'd never seen it before and let out an involuntary "Wow!" when I saw a carmine red Lotus Emira. There was nothing erotic about the conversation on the drive home. They talked mainly about their home, how happy they were in it, and what a good deal they'd gotten on it. When we arrived in a tree-lined avenue, I had to suppress another wow as we went up a long driveway to a house with a double garage and eight windows along the front. No one would have guessed anything unusual was going on behind the sober green front door.

Ray directed me to the couch and Angie pointedly sat beside me, so close her right thigh brushed against my left. The first touch of body parts went through me like electricity. I must admit to feeling a little nervous at this point. I was cottoning on to what they wanted. I was on board but wasn't sure how it was going to work. Ray poured us each a glass of Scotch, without asking if we wanted one. Scotch isn't normally my drink, but I'd been on my feet all evening and John had a strict no drinking on the job policy. We all clinked glasses. I took a big gulp and immediately felt more confident things would play out well, one way or another. Angie put her glass down, grabbed my collar, and pulled me to her aggressively. She'd always seemed a little reserved. Her lips were suddenly moving against mine. I was surprised by the speed of it, but keen to respond. One thing I wanted to do was check how Ray was taking it. If this was Angie's way of taking revenge on him for something, I might turn round to see him pointing a gun at me. What he was actually doing was sitting in the armchair opposite, grinning broadly with his drink in his lap, like he was enjoying a show. I took this to be a green light and went for it. I unbuttoned Angie's blouse to reveal her small, perky tits in a black silk bra. I was about to reach behind her back to undo it when she pushed me away. Putting her hands on my shoulders, she shoved me against the back of the couch. It had the effect she wanted of giving her access to my belt buckle. She undid it quickly and soon had my work pants open with my boxers exposed. She pulled down the top of my shorts and my erect cock sprang out. She bent to put her lips around it. I gasped, partly with pleasure but also with surprise. It was all happening so fast. We'd gone from the first kiss to my cock in her mouth in less than a minute. A lot of the girls I'd known before had been shy and had needed to be coaxed out of their clothes. Sometimes it had taken more than an hour. Angie's urgency felt almost like an attack. After two minutes of vigorous sucking, she pulled her mouth away from my cock and attached her hand to the base. Moving to the side so Ray could have a better view, she told him, "It's much bigger than yours, darling. It tastes so good, too."

Ray was breathing heavily. "Are you saying Mark's dick is better than mine, Angie?"

"I didn't want to be the one to say it but, yes, Mark's dick is a lot better than yours, Ray." He let out a low groan and undid his fly. I thought he was going to demonstrate how much worse his cock was, but he just started edging. This was my first direct experience of a man getting his greatest pleasure from watching his partner with another man. At the time, I couldn't see what was in it for him. He obviously loved Angie and was passionately attracted to her, so why didn't he fuck her himself? I didn't have much time to contemplate this as Angie was onto her next move. Standing up, she put both hands under her skirt and pulled down her panties in a quick, efficient movement. There was something contemptuous in the way she threw them at—rather than to—Ray with the words, "See how wet your wife is for the young man with the hot dick."

She hitched her skirt to her thighs but didn't take it off. Straddling me, she lowered herself onto my cock. She must have had a lot of practice at this because her aim was perfect. There was a momentary tickle of pubes against my cockhead and then my whole shaft was engulfed in the moist heat of her cunt. It wasn't my first time by any means but I was still comparatively inexperienced back then. I leaned back, closed my eyes, and enjoyed the feeling of being inside Angie. Opening my eyes again, I saw Ray over her shoulder. He was gazing at us fixedly, massaging the tip of his cock between his finger and thumb. His cock was only about three inches long and didn't look hard at all. Later, I understood that years of masturbating instead of fucking had made erections unnecessary. His cock had been trained to stay soft. As I looked at him and felt his wife moving up and down on me, I had a feeling of superiority. He had a fast car and a big house but I was the alpha male here. I was the one enjoying his wife's pussy while he jerked off like a dirty little schoolboy. I looked at him, opened my mouth, and let my eyes roll back, showing him how it felt to fuck his wife. He looked back and said, "She's damn good, isn't she?" I wasn't sure how to reply so I nodded.

Angie said, "Not that Ray would know. He hasn't been inside me for years."

"Slut," said Ray.

"Wimp," she replied.

This exchange of sweet nothings kicked them both to the next level of excitement. He pulled his cock harder and faster while she drove herself down onto my cock with renewed force. As her breathing quickened, I knew she was going to cum soon. I had to hold on. When she shouted, "Fuck, yes!" and her cunt contracted around my cock, I waited to see if she was going to climb off me. She didn't so I reckoned it was okay to cum inside her. These days, I'd hold out longer and make sure she was completely satisfied. Back then, I pulled her close to me and felt my cock shooting my seed up her. I couldn't resist giving Ray a wink as I came inside his wife. This pushed him over the edge. It was about as close as you could get to a simultaneous orgasm with three people in the room.

Angie lifted herself off me and stood up. She smoothed her skirt demurely and handed me a tissue. After wiping my cock and doing my pants back up, I sat back and waited to see what would happen next. I assumed we'd have a drink and a chat about what had happened. "Well," said Angie, "we mustn't keep you."

"Popular guy like you," added Ray. "You must have hundreds of demands on your time."

I must admit to feeling slightly used. I'd done my job and now they wanted me out of their respectable house before the neighbors noticed anything. Ray showed me to the door. He didn't offer to drive me home so I had to walk. On the way back, any hurt feelings melted away. It had been an evening of self-discovery. Fucking a woman who was in love with someone else had been the most intense sexual experience of my life. After that, being with a single girl would lack flavor.

FIVE

PETER

THE WELCOME PACK INCLUDED A MAP of the campus and a letter from the computer science department's admin team telling me to be at the Lovelace Building at nine o'clock. I got lost a couple of times and it was a quarter past nine before I ran into the building's hallway, hot and flustered. Only one person was there—Sophie. "You're late!" she chided me. She pinned a badge with my name on it to the lapel of my jacket and we went into the main lecture theater, where the other students were already gathered. The professor looked up at us sourly as we slipped into the back row. I tried to concentrate on what he was saying about the course, but I was filled with gratitude for Sophie. On her first full day at college—a stressful time for anyone—she'd thought of me. I was also aware how much I was sweating, sitting right next to her. I tried not to smell by the sheer force of my will. We spent the day meeting the tutors and touring the department. Sophie and I were together all the time, whispering an ironic commentary on events into each other's ears. We lunched together but, in the evening, she went to her block and I went to mine. As I walked back alone, the main feeling I had was happiness that I had a friend. I suspected Mark would be off doing his own thing most of the time. In Sophie, I'd maybe found the person most crucial to my wellbeing - someone who'd hang out with me in preference to anyone else.

Sophie and I had an unspoken agreement to be each other's wingman, or wingperson, to follow the college's policy of political correctness. Whenever there was a meeting, seminar, party, or any of the other get-togethers designed to embarrass shy people, we went together. It spared us both the mortification of walking into a room alone. People got used to seeing us together and assumed we were a couple. Sophie was amused by this idea. If anyone asked if I was her boyfriend, she replied, "No, that's just Peter." I wasn't too worried about being friend zoned. It was a whole lot better than the no-friends zone.

One day, we were walking to the shops when the realization struck us that we were holding hands. "Do we always do this?" asked Sophie.

"I'm not sure," I confessed. "I don't think so."

"Is this the first time?"

"Not sure about that, either." Her hand was still in mine. Despite her surprise, she hadn't pulled it away. "It feels nice, though."

"It's not horrendous," she admitted. We carried on walking, our hands still together. After that, it seemed natural to hold hands. I hoped this meant she was now my girlfriend, but I didn't want to say anything. I liked holding her hand and I was afraid it might stop if I assumed anything from it. It was the only couply thing we did for some time. We didn't even kiss good night and I called her Sophie, instead of honeybunch or my sugar plum. This went on for a couple of weeks. Then, one afternoon, we were sitting on a bench. Money was tight for both of us: it comes with the territory when you're a student. We were sharing one ice cream cone to save the pennies, passing it from hand to hand between licks. I enjoyed putting my tongue where hers had just been. I wondered if it was the closest we'd ever get to kissing. When we were down to a dry cone, she turned to me and asked, "Peter, what are we?"

I was still afraid any answer might ruin whatever it was we had so I deflected her question with a quip. "Two souls in a goldfish bowl," I hazarded, misquoting a song we both liked.

She punched me lightly on the upper arm. (I didn't think much about this at the time, but certainly came back to it later.) "Be serious."

Still picking my words carefully, I said, "We're good friends." Before she could ask me to elaborate, I asked her, "Do you think we'll ever be more than that?"

She bit her lip and looked away. "It's what I'm wondering. I mean, we hang out together a lot. You're the first person I want to talk to about my day. If I had any sort of problem, I don't see why I'd go to anyone other than you."

I took a deep breath and spoke with a little chuckle in my voice, hoping I could pass it off as a joke if she didn't take it the right way. "So . . . it's almost like we're boyfriend and girlfriend."

"I guess," she said, looking at the ground, thoughtfully. "The only difference is we don't get naked together."

"Would it be so terrible if we did?"

She shuddered. "My body is hideous. I keep my eyes shut in the shower so I don't have to see all the sprouting and oozing bits."

With an understanding nod, I said, "I spent some time as an exhibition at Ripley's Believe It or Not. I stood there naked and people marveled at how the Almighty could commit such an atrocity." She laughed, which I took as a good sign. I decided to try my luck. "Wouldn't we be doing the rest of the world a favor if we got naked together rather than inflicting our bodies on anyone else?"

"Possibly the worst pick up line ever," she said. After a pause, which seemed to last several hours but was probably less than a minute, she added, "It might have worked, though."

On the way home, we graduated from holding hands to walking arm in arm. I dared to hope she'd invite me in when we arrived back at her building, but she simply said, "Good night, Peter. We'll talk about this more tomorrow. I'll come over at two o'clock."

It worried me a little that she still thought we had things to talk about, but I went to the pad feeling optimistic. I sat at the desk in my bedroom trying to work on an assignment but couldn't concentrate. I wanted to knock on Sophie's door and suggest we spend the evening together. Something told me it was a bad idea. I'd read enough articles about relationships to be familiar with such concepts as space and smothering. At ten o'clock, I went to bed because it felt like the normal thing to do, but I was sure I wouldn't sleep. The prospect of having a real live girlfriend was keeping the adrenaline flowing too fast.

Hours went by as I imagined being with Sophie. My lurid fantasies weren't exactly appropriate to have about someone who was technically still my friend. Other thoughts were more romantic than sexual. I pictured what it would be like if Sophie and I got married. A woman like her wouldn't look right in a white, lacy wedding dress. Maybe I'd see a gothic vision in a black and purple gown coming up the aisle toward me. I had a feeling our children would be geeky and wondered what I could do to stop them being bullied at school. I was getting ahead of myself over a girl I'd never even kissed, but sleepless nights take the mind to strange places.

At two in the morning, I remembered her saying she'd come over at two o'clock. I'd assumed she meant two in the afternoon, but if she wanted a nighttime tryst, I wasn't going to disappoint her. I went out into the den and opened the main door of the pad, in case she was waiting outside. She wasn't of course and I went back to bed feeling foolish.

I replayed her punching my arm. Feeling the place where her fist had landed, I was disappointed there was no bruise. I would have liked to reignite the pain with my fingers, not that there'd been much pain. It had only been a playful tap. I'd never had masochistic fantasies before, but I had a vivid image of myself chained in the middle of a room with Sophie walking round me, punching parts of my body as she pleased. If I begged her to stop, would she? Or would it make her go at me even harder? What had I done to deserve this treatment? It was hard to believe I'd cheated on her. Maybe my body had disappointed her so much she had to punish me for it.

I must have fallen asleep eventually, because I woke up at eleven in the morning to a silent pad. Mark had gone out, which was a relief. He'd seen me with Sophie a couple of times and had been encouraging, saying, "She looks like a nice person. Go for it." I wanted them to meet at some point, but not now. This was one time when two people needed to be alone.

I cleaned the den and even tidied up my bedroom in a spirit of optimism. At ten to two, I went to the kitchenette and turned the kettle on to make some tea. I looked through the cupboard. Entertaining a lady felt like an occasion for fine bone china, but the cupboard was full of mismatching mugs left behind by previous residents. I found a couple of sachets of sugar and a little jug, which I filled with milk. It wasn't the elegant tea party I'd been aiming for, but I hoped she'd appreciate the effort. When everything was as prepared as I could manage, I sat and waited, hoping the tea wouldn't get cold.

There was a knock at the door. I opened it and blushed as I saw Sophie again. It was hard to reconcile the dominatrix sex goddess of my night visions with the nice girl standing in front of me. She was wearing a floral print blouse, jeans, and white basketball boots rather than a black basque and patent leather stilettos. We stood in the doorway for longer than normal. We weren't sure how to greet each other. Did we kiss now? If so, how? A chaste peck on the cheek or a tongue down the throat? We settled for a brief hug.

We sat down and I served the tea. We blew into our cups to cover the uncomfortable silence. I was reluctant to have one of our regular conversations about films, music, or our studies. I had a feeling it would send me scurrying back to the friend zone, and I didn't want to settle for that anymore. Finally, she said, "I've been thinking about what we said last night." When women thought about me, they usually decided to run in the opposite direction. Relief and delight flooded over me with her next words. "Let's give it a go."

"That's wonderful," I replied. It wasn't the smoothest thing I could have said, but I had no idea what I was doing. Nor did she, apparently. We sat in silence for another minute. Was this my cue to pick her up and carry her to my bed in a caveman fashion? Somehow, I couldn't see myself doing that.

"Don't make me regret this, Peter," she said. "Be nice to me."

"Hey, I made you tea."

"You did. Good start. I will want tea every day going forwards."

"You've got it."

There was another short silence, then she looked at me with a knowing smile. "I suppose if we're going to be romantically entwined, we should talk about the S word." I was more than happy to talk about sex. I hoped she'd be more explicit and call it something other than the S word. "How many lucky ladies have enjoyed the pleasures of Peter's bed?"

My fragile male ego was telling me to lie, "Well, you know, I stopped counting after the first hundred. After a while, they all blend into one. Get 'em in, screw 'em senseless, send 'em on their way. That's how I roll, sweetheart."

I had a feeling she wasn't going to buy that, so I said, "It's a nice round number. The roundest of all numbers. Zero."

"It's nothing to be ashamed of," she said, showing men and women think very differently on this subject. "You've been saving yourself for the right person. Who knows? That person might not be too far away from you now."

I didn't want to tell her I hadn't so much been saving myself as coping with industrial strength indifference from the girls I met. My heart beat faster as I asked her, "What about you?"

"I suppose if we're going to be together, we should be completely honest with each other."

"Yes, we should. Completely."

She leaned across and clasped my hands between hers. "Last summer, I took a job in a factory that made double-glazed window units. I spent the morning loading units onto a conveyor belt and the afternoon taking units off the conveyor belt so you can see it was a job with plenty of variety. I went home exhausted from standing up for eight hours and with my clothes covered in this horrible black sealant they used to hold the units together. It was like tar. Once it got on your clothes, it never came off. Anyway, Daniel, one of the supervisors must have thought I was cute or funny or maybe just easy. He promised to show me a better life. He took me away from the conveyor belt and into the office, where I spent my time sitting at a computer processing the orders so the guys knew how many units to ship out. I went home with legs which weren't aching and clothes not coated in black sticky stuff. One Friday evening, Daniel asked if I fancied a drink after work. He took me to a bar and bought me a glass of wine. I noticed he was only drinking Coke. He said he was driving and asked if I'd like to go for a spin. Well, the drive happened to take us back to his apartment. He invited me in for another drink and we ended up doing the wicked deed. I didn't tell him it was my first time. I tried to act like I was well-versed in such matters without coming across too slutty. He offered to drive me home every evening with a short detour to his place. We both knew the affair wasn't going to last any longer than my job there. I guess in a way he was using me, but I was using him as well. I figured I had to start somewhere down the path of sexual awakening so it might as well be there. I've no bad feelings toward Daniel. I wasn't doing anything I didn't want to do. Well, there was one thing but never mind about that now. He was older than me, but not in an icky way. Only a couple of years. Well, there you have it. Declare me to be the whore of Babylon and tell me never to darken your doors again."

I didn't do that. Instead, I said, "It's better if one of us knows what they're doing."

She stood up and reached for my hand. "Take me to your bed," she said. In fact, *she* took *me*, but it wasn't the time to quibble about that.

Before closing the door to my room, I put a tie on the handle. I didn't think Mark would come barging in but I wanted to impress him. Sophie lay on the bed, still fully clothed. I lay beside her and put my arm around her middle, below the breasts. My heart was thumping so loud, I was afraid she'd hear and realize how nervous I was. I felt like I was serving for the Wimbledon title or looking at the final putt to win the US Masters. All I had to do was hold my nerve and I could do something extraordinary. "Er . . . Sophie?" I began.

"Yes."

"Would it be okay if I kissed you?"

She laughed. "How delightfully old-fashioned. Next, you'll be asking my father if you can pay your respects to me."

"People are always going on about the importance of consent in matters sexual."

"Yes, you're right. Peter, I hereby give you free rein over my body. If you do anything wrong, I'll say no or slug you, but either way, you'll know. Now kiss me, you crazy fool."

We often think kissing is something we're born knowing how to do, but it's like driving. Experienced people make it look effortless but it's complicated for the beginner. I'd seen it done in films and knew the essentials of putting one pair of lips against another. I put my mouth to Sophie's, but our lips were so dry it was like rubbing two pieces of sandpaper together. We both licked our lips and tried again. It was better. Her lips were beautifully soft on mine. She made almost inaudible grunts as we kissed. I hoped this was a sign of pleasure rather than irritation. I had some idea that tongues were an optional extra as the kiss became more passionate. I flicked my tongue at her lips a couple of times like a snake tasting the air. She didn't seem repelled and opened her mouth a little. The first touch of our tongues made the blood throb in my ears. I couldn't believe a girl was allowing me to be so intimate with her and I didn't even have to pay. The relief and gratitude I felt were so overwhelming, I almost cried. I thought it would freak Sophie out if kissing made me weep so I held back my tears. As Sophie opened her mouth more, her jaw cracked. She hadn't opened her mouth so wide for a while. Maybe she and her summertime love hadn't done much kissing.

We did nothing but kiss for twenty minutes. I didn't want it to stop. Kissing a girl was hugely preferable to not kissing one. I thought someone should make the next move, but I didn't know what that next move was. I was right in that she had a better idea of what to do than I did. Her hand snaked up my t-shirt, stroked over my belly, and found my left nipple. She ran her finger around it and dragged her thumbnail across it, making my balls tingle. Even then I found it hard to live in the moment. Where could this scene go next? If she was touching my nipple, it stood to reason I could touch hers, right? That seemed only fair. I undid the first button of her blouse. I felt like a boy opening a parcel on Christmas morning. I was unwrapping her slowly, letting the anticipation build. I didn't want to see my present too early. I revealed her throat and part of her upper chest, but nothing that looked like true breast. I didn't want to come across as too single minded, only interested in a few small parts of her, so I kissed her throat and along her collar bone. The appreciative little moans and squeaks told me I was doing something right. Undoing the next button, I saw some swelling and the top of her bra. It was a simple white cotton bra, but I'd never seen anything more erotic in my life. She wasn't raising any objections to my exposing her, so I undid another button and saw the unmistakable roundness of two breasts. I popped open the final button and pushed her blouse aside. I still wanted to show I was interested in her as a whole person, so I kissed her concave belly. I couldn't ignore the two stars of the show for long. I kissed her breasts through the bra. My lips found her nipples under the cotton and I was excited to feel how hard they were. I tentatively hooked my thumb under the right cup of her bra. Looking up at her face, I didn't see any alarm. Her eyes were closed, which made me wonder briefly if she was picturing someone else. She was smiling quietly, which I assumed meant she was happy about what was going on. Like I was lifting the veil on some newly acquired treasure, I peeled the right cup of her bra up toward her shoulder while still watching her face for any signs of disapproval. I was almost afraid to look down. When I did, I gasped. I'd spent a good part of the night before wondering what Sophie's breasts were like. I'd seen enough photos of different breasts to know there were several variations on the theme. Would her nipples be a vivid purple, quiet pink, or warm brown? Would the surrounding aureole stand out in stark contrast to the rest of the breast or be almost the same color? The real thing was beyond all my dreams. Even pushed out of shape by the underwire of her bra pressing down on it, her right breast looked perfect. A small, round caramel-colored orb with the most subtle darkening of shade at the aureole and a brown nut of a nipple.

As I admired her breast, I felt something move inside my groin. I'd hoped this first experience of being with Sophie was just beginning and I did not want it to finish. I'd happily have spent the rest of my life lying there, exploring her body. All other hopes, dreams, and ambitions had evaporated. Nothing mattered except this woman who, against all the odds, was in my bed. I clenched every muscle I could find, but it was like trying to hold the sea back with one hand. Cum shot into my shorts, but I felt no pleasure or release. I was embarrassed at my lack of control and disappointed the feeling of breathless excitement had flowed out of me along with my seed.

I hoped I'd recover quickly and get the feeling back, so I kissed her belly and hoped she wouldn't notice. She sensed immediately something had changed. "What happened?" she asked. I didn't have time to come up with a face-saving answer before she bit her lip. She knew enough about men to work out the problem. "Oh, baby," she said, putting her arms around my neck and pulling her head into her bosom. Even in my post-orgasmic funk, my face against her breasts made me feel faint. "It's okay," she continued. "I take it as a huge compliment that I excite you so much." I assumed we'd lie there until my equipment reset itself, then carry on where we'd left off. Unfortunately, she had other ideas. "Are you hungry?" she asked. I had no desire ever to eat again. Sexual arousal would give my body all the sustenance it needed for the rest of my life. "I could go a pizza." How could anyone think about pizza at a time like this? What I wanted from her was some acknowledgement life would never be the same now I'd seen a breast. Maybe she didn't appreciate how momentous a moment it was for me. She was lucky enough to be able to see her breasts any time she liked.

We got dressed and walked to the Italian restaurant, holding hands unselfconsciously. It was nice. Her hand felt good in mine. I also felt some pride and wanted people to see me walking with a woman.

Despite everything we'd said and done during the afternoon, there was a word I wanted to hear from Sophie's mouth. "Are you my girlfriend?" I asked.

"No, I'm your concubine. This afternoon will cost you two camels and a goat."

"I left them in my other jacket. I'll pay you later."

She stopped walking, turned, and looked up at me. "Of course I'm your girlfriend, you idiot." A look of insecurity flashed across her face. "If that's what you want, of course."

"It's definitely what I want." We kissed, a long, tender kiss on the lips. She had said the word I needed to hear and I felt something which might have been the first stirrings of love.

I ate my pizza quickly and refused Sophie's suggestion of sharing a slice of chocolate cake. I wanted to get back to my room as soon as possible. My hope was we were taking a break to refuel before going back to bed. Walking back, I was disappointed when she turned her steps toward her building instead of mine. I remained hopeful we'd go up to her room. "Today's been amazing," she said. I was so glad to hear that. I was focusing more on the premature ending than all the amazing parts. My hopes were dashed by her next words. "See you tomorrow."

"Well . . . I could come up if you want," I said, as casually as I could manage. "I'm in no rush or anything."

"I've got an assignment to write. The deadline's in two days and I'm not half done yet."

Two days? That meant she had all of tomorrow. It sounded a pretty lame excuse for not inviting me up. I looked at her face. It would have been better if I'd seen some playful cruelty in her eyes, showing she knew how desperate I was and enjoyed leaving me frustrated. I didn't see any of that. She was going back to her room alone because she wanted to work on her assignment. While I wasn't sure I'd ever think about anything except sex ever again, her mind was on something else. We kissed on the lips and she went inside. I walked back to the pad. I hoped no one could see the bulge in my pants but, at the same time, I kind of hoped people could see it.

Six

PETER

WHEN I GOT BACK TO THE pad, I found Mark in the den. He was sat in one of the easy chairs, watching TV with a can of beer in his hand. "You don't look too happy," he said. "Grab a couple more beers and talk to me."

I was tempted. Maybe Mark knew the magic words needed to make a woman forget about her work and run back to her boyfriend's bed. I decided not to, though. I wanted to brag about being in bed with a woman but couldn't bear to admit how it had ended. At the least he'd smirk and my ego had been on enough of a rollercoaster for one day. I got him another beer from the fridge before going into my room and shutting the door.

I lay on my bed, not sure whether to masturbate or not. Were my days of jerking off over? Should I save all my sexual energy for when I was with Sophie? I decided there wasn't much danger of me being so spent I couldn't get it up. I was more concerned my penis would never go down again. My problem was the dreaded premature ejaculation. If I came a couple of times before I saw her again, I'd be less excitable and better able to control myself. Unfortunately, my first thoughts weren't arousing. I faced another feverish night as a virgin. At least, I was probably still a virgin. What was the exact second at which virginity was officially lost? Did cumming in my pants while in the presence of a semi-naked woman constitute losing it? I wasn't sure and, to be honest, I'm still not. If I'd asked Mark, he'd have said I needed to complete the sexual act. In other words, I was a virgin until I came inside someone. Years later, I was talking to my friend Simon, who's gay. He and his partner, Will, have been together more than twenty years. Simon was well into his second bottle of wine and revealed more than he intended, but he told me he and Will had never penetrated each other. All the sex they had was in the form of hand and blow jobs. It seemed odd to say two men who had enjoyed an active sex life over many years were still virgins. Maybe you're no longer a virgin when you've engaged in a sexual act with another person that left you satisfied.

This was not the case for me. I had been so close and my body had let me down. I was mad at my cock. If he'd controlled himself for a few more minutes, he might have had a warm, moist vagina to ejaculate into. If that had happened, I would have lost my virginity beyond all reasonable doubt and I would have been feeling so much happier with myself.

It wasn't long until my thoughts took a brighter turn. The vision of Sophie's breast loomed up in my mind. I was struck again by how perfect it was. The size, shape, and color palette were all beyond reproach. I planned in great detail what I'd do next time I saw it and—hopefully—its twin sister. I wanted to lick them all over. The most potent image I had was one of those nut-brown nipples in my mouth. I badly wanted to suck both of them. That thought pushed me over the edge and made me cum into a tissue.

Faced with another post-orgasmic ebb of hormones, I became anxious. Did I have any right to assume there'd be a next time? Maybe Sophie was in her own bed having reflections of her own. Perhaps she was appalled she'd allowed someone like me to touch her and was determined it must never happen again. The scene played out clearly in my head.

There's a knock at the door. Sophie comes in but without the energy of someone in a new relationship. She looks sad. "Hey, what's wrong?" I ask, with a knot of fear already in my stomach.

"Peter," she begins, "I like you." I've heard this speech often enough to know what the next word will be. "But I think we'll both admit what happened yesterday was a mistake." I will admit no such thing. What happened yesterday was the greatest moment of my life, easily outstripping all the other moments put together. "It would be better if we went back to being friends." I agree of course. Having Sophie as a friend is better than not having her in my life at all, but it's a hundred times worse than having her as my girlfriend. Anyone who's seen me holding her hand will see us standing apart in future and realize what a loser I am.

Fortunately, these reflections didn't last long. As my cock came back to life, my erotic thoughts went in a more twisted direction. Sophie had been lovely with me when I'd had my unfortunate incident. Maybe she wasn't feeling so sympathetic now. During the night she'd gotten angry with me for failing to satisfy her as a real man should. She had decided I needed to be punished for my shortcomings.

There's a knock at the door. Sophie comes in, looking stern. She orders me to take off all my clothes and lie on my front. She stays fully-dressed apart from her right shoe which she takes off and dangles in front of my face. "Kiss it," she commands.

"It's a bit dirty," I protest.

"Lick it clean." After I've licked her shoe clean, she jerks it away from my face. Kneeling up on the bed, she lays her shoe across my naked buttocks. I know what's coming next and brace myself. She brings her shoe crashing down on my pale defenseless ass. "What do you say?" she asks.

"Thank you for punishing me," I reply. "I deserve it for cumming too quickly."

"Damn right you deserve it," she says and proceeds to beat my butt another eleven times. I think that's the end of it but she turns me onto my back and takes something out of her pocket. I can't see

it clearly at first because it's only a couple of inches long. Maybe it's a love bullet and I wonder what she's going to do with it. She brings it closer to my face and I realize it's actually a red chili. She touches the pointy end to my lips. "Bite it in half," she says. I do what I'm told, thinking there might be some symbolism at play here. "Swallow," she adds. I gulp down the inch of raw chili, assuming the burning in my mouth and throat is the punishment. I haven't figured on Sophie's sadistic imagination. She holds the fresh cut chili in her right hand and my cock in her left. Carefully, she runs the juicy end of the chili along the shaft of my cock and onto my ball sack. She kneels back on her heels and waits. For a moment, I feel nothing. Maybe my cock has natural immunity to capsaicin. Then it hits me. Starting as warmth, it soon develops into unbearable, stinging heat coupled with a panic that I must do something—put cold water on it, stick my dick in the fridge, anything to stop the chemical corrosion going on in my most sensitive parts. It's not possible, though. Sophie keeps me in place by hugging me—a loving act of cruelty.

This image was so overpowering that I made a decision. Next time I saw Sophie, I'd ask her to punish me. I came for the second time. I don't remember much else so I must have gone to sleep.

When I woke up the next morning, I forewent my usual tea in favor of a strong coffee. This promised to be an important day and I needed to be sharp. I regretted lying awake so long in a daze of fantasies. I needed to go to the shop and the fresh air helped me wake up. I bought two cans of Coke and a box of Sophie's favorite chocolates. Back in the pad, I changed my sheets and carefully secreted the night's used tissues at the bottom of my wastepaper basket. In the cold light of day, it didn't seem such a good idea to offer Sophie my naked body and beg her to hurt me. Again, I wondered why my mind had gone to such a strange place during the night.

I jumped when I heard the knock at the door. I opened it to find Sophie outside. I didn't see vengeful fury in her eyes. Equally, I didn't see the sad but resolute look of a woman about to dump someone. She simply looked happy to see me. I had to remind myself once more that she wasn't just the sex siren and sadist of my dreams. She was my nerdy girlfriend—pretty, sexy, but a real person. I thought it better if my first words were not about sex. "Did you get your assignment finished?" I asked.

She sat on one of the easy chairs in the den and puffed out her cheeks. "Eventually, yes," she said. "It took me half the night and then I lay in bed wondering if I should change parts of it." Strangely, I'd neglected academic work the night before. "Did you sleep well?" she asked.

"Not bad," I lied. Immediately, I felt guilty as we'd promised to be completely honest with each other.

"You mean you didn't lie awake all night thinking of me?" she asked, with a mischievous grin.

She had no idea how true that was. "Maybe for a while," I replied, airily.

"I've been thinking a lot about you, as well."

"In a good way?"

"In a very good way. You were so sweet and gentle with me, you made me feel loved, even if . . . things finished a bit sooner than we expected."

"Yes, sorry about that."

"Don't worry. I've heard it happens to all men from time to time."

"Did it ever happen with the guy from the glass factory?" Even as I was speaking, I knew I shouldn't ask such a question.

She didn't seem to notice how inappropriate I was being and looked almost apologetic as she said, "Well, no, but he was a bit older, more experienced."

I was surprised to realize part of me wanted her to tell me outright that he was better than me. I didn't know why I'd feel like that. The more sensible part of me understood I'd gotten away with asking one question about him and shouldn't push my luck. Besides, there was something I wanted to ask above all else. "Could we possibly try it again some time?"

"I certainly wouldn't rule it out."

"When were you thinking?"

"I was thinking maybe Tuesday next week or . . . I don't know how you're fixed, but I'm free right now."

"Works for me."

Sophie led me into my bedroom again. She took off her clothes. It wasn't like she was doing a striptease or anything. She did it in a matter-of-fact way like she was about to go swimming. She didn't even look at me while she was doing it. It was like I was seeing into her private world. The voyeuristic element made the casual reveal of her body even more arousing. When she'd finished undressing, she stood by the bed, neither showing off nor covering up. It was the first time I'd seen her—or any other woman, for that matter—naked. I was pleased to note her left breast was every inch the equal of her right. To me, they were both the ideal shape and size. Her stomach was flat. A lot of men would have balked at the thick, dark hair between her legs, but I liked it. It was like a curtain discreetly hiding the inner sanctum. I looked forward to discovering what secrets lay behind. She let me look at her for a while, then said, "Your turn." I tried to match her nonchalance in undressing, but my hands were shaking as I unbuttoned my shirt. I had a fear she'd see me standing nude in front of her and realize her mistake. Looking me up and down, she'd say, "Is that the time? I must get going." I stepped out of my shoes, took my shirt off, unbuckled my trousers, and slid them down my legs. "Don't forget to take off your socks," said Sophie. I would have remembered without the prompt. I'd read a few women's magazines and knew it was impossible for a man to be attractive while naked in socks. I stood there, feeling like I was at an audition. Would I get the part of Sophie's long-term sex partner? Obviously, my main concern was what she'd think of my penis. Men often kid themselves about their pride and joy, but I try to be honest. My cock maxes out at a slender five inches. It's maybe not the smallest in the world but it's not going to win any awards. I admitted to myself early on in life that I'd need to work on my personality because I couldn't rely on women being stunned by the sheer magnitude of my dick. Unsurprisingly, it was fully erect so showing itself at its best. Sophie's jaw didn't hit the floor when she saw it but she said, "Not bad," and looked relieved as if it was better than she expected. She wasn't nearly as relieved as I was. It seemed I'd at least achieved a pass mark. She lay on the bed and beckoned me to join her.

My heart was beating fast. I tried to keep my excitement under control. I didn't want to risk another premature ending. It was still overwhelming to realize I was in bed with a real woman. To start with, we kissed. We'd done that before. It was a good way of easing back into things. I heard music playing somewhere along the corridor. I used it as a timekeeping device. While this song was playing, I wouldn't do more than kiss her. There was a pause and another song started. This was my cue to kiss her neck. I quickly learned this had to be done assertively. If I was too tentative, it tickled and made her giggle. When I went in harder, her sighs and moans suggested I was doing something right. When there was another pause in the music, I gently placed Sophie's hands on the pillow above her head. I gasped as I saw her armpits. They weren't body parts I'd thought much about. I hadn't seen them as having any more erotic potential than knees or ankles. What made Sophie's armpits so intriguing was the hair. It was as thick and dark as her pubes. Kissing them tickled my nose. She'd put on some deodorant. It was chalky on my lips and didn't taste nice. Some sweat had broken through the protective layer. People go to great lengths to cover up their natural aromas but Sophie's sweat made my cock throb. My studious girl had this animalistic side to her—a body pumping out pheromones to attract men. When she realized what I was seeing, she clamped her arms to her sides. "I shaved them in the summer when I was . . . you know. I haven't touched them since. I assumed no one else would see them. Do you mind?"

I knew already I didn't mind at all, but I said, "I'd better have a closer look." There was a roguish twinkle in her eye as she put her arms behind her head. She was showing a part of herself she normally kept private. "Does all that hair . . . make you smell?" I asked, quietly.

"Not real . . ." she began, before looking closely at my face and deciding to change course. "Oh yes, sometimes I stink. I wake up in the morning and my whole bedroom smells of my hairy, sweaty armpits."

My breathing was getting quicker and my erection was digging into her thigh. I knew I couldn't take much more of this. "Okay, Sophie, that'll do."

She was enjoying my torment too much to stop. "If I walked into a room full of men, not one of them could resist my scent. I'd be too much woman for them." It was the first time she talked about using her body to excite other men, rather than me. It triggered something inside me I hadn't expected. I didn't have time to tense my muscles. My cum shot out of me onto the sheet below. I thought some of it had splashed her thigh so there wasn't any point covering it up. "Already?" was all she said, with a raise of her eyebrows.

"Sorry about that, but I've bought snacks." I didn't mean to come out with such a non-sequitur. My reason for buying the Coke and chocolates was to keep Sophie in my bed. I figured if she had food there, she'd be less likely to suggest going for pizza. She seemed happy with the arrangement and sat up in bed to open her can. She took a chocolate out of the box, licked the bottom of it, and rubbed it on her left nipple. "Suck," she said. Lying beside her, I craned my neck up. She leaned forward and offered her breast to my mouth. To me, her whole body tasted great without any topping, but there was something supremely sensuous about tasting something rich and sweet while sucking on a nipple. It's probably best not to delve too deeply into the psychological implications of that one. I licked under her left breast, tasting the salty tang of her sweat after the sweetness of chocolate. My cock was showing a keen interest in what was going on. It was time to try again.

The music was still playing in the other room. I wasn't sure if I should allocate the length of one song to each breast or to both of them. After the song changed, I decided it was time to move on. Kissing her abdomen after her breasts felt a bit like the support act coming back on after a couple of numbers from the headliners. I felt the hard oblong of her abdominal muscles through her skin. Her bellybutton was a surprisingly rich source of erotic potential. Despite her slender frame, her bellybutton was deep, moist with sweat, and had a scent that can only be described as asshole lite. I dipped the tip of my tongue into it, which made her moan quietly.

There was a longer gap before the next song. When it began the music sounded different, so I guessed the album had been changed. I decided to save the best for last. With a great show of restraint, I bypassed her crotch and moved onto her thighs, which had a pleasing softness. She walked everywhere but it's not like she worked out or anything. Her legs were shapely but not muscly. I kissed my way down them until I got to her feet.

"Not my feet," she said, laughing with a mixture of fun and embarrassment. "They stink."

I kissed her soles and put each of her toes in turn into my mouth. "Yes, they do," I told her, although I'd have said they were aromatic rather than stinking. "I like it." I immediately regretted saying that. The last thing I wanted was her storming out because I'd revealed one perversion too far. I held my breath in anticipation.

"Noted," was the only thing she said with another laugh.

I kissed her feet until the end of the next song, wondering why I was so turned on by them. It was another body part I hadn't considered before. The smell of female—in all its varieties—was speaking to something primitive in my brain.

I kissed my way back up her legs. When my head was level with her pussy, I kissed Sophie's pubes while breathing in heavily through my nose. Her pussy had the most complex scent I'd encountered so far. With every inhalation, I was aware of a different note. There was sweat, piss, perfume, soap, and the laundered cotton of her panties. It reminded me of my first glass of wine. I didn't immediately know if I liked it, but I knew it was something interesting I wanted to explore. If pussies smelled of roses, we'd love them at first but we'd get bored of them more easily. My thumbs tried to find a path through her pubes. Confronted with the various ridges and promontories of Sophie's vulva, I was confused. In the porn magazines I'd studied, the vaginal entrance was normally spread wide and inviting. I couldn't see that Sophie had any such entrance. Just my luck to hook up with a woman who didn't have a vagina. I realized it must be hidden behind one of the folds. I decided to lick what I could see before going any deeper. My plan was to use my tongue on her until she came. She couldn't claim I'd left her unsatisfied even if I came in a second. I licked the most prominent part of her vulva. Using the flat of my tongue, I covered as wide an area as possible to maximize my chances of hitting the right spot. Fortunately, I didn't have to work unsupervised. "Up a bit," said Sophie. She put both hands on her pussy and spread her lips. I was delighted to find a vagina was indeed hiding behind them. "Get your tongue in there. To the right, no I meant my right. A little bit faster. No! Don't move! I'll tell you when to move." This was a side to Sophie I hadn't seen much of before. She could be bossy to get her own way. I didn't mind. There was something erotic about being in bed with a woman who knew what she wanted. I did not move. My tongue stayed in the exact spot she'd directed me to. I still wasn't entirely sure what I was doing. I didn't know how to move my tongue—up and down, side to side, or in circles? None of this had been covered in sex education class at my school. I listened to the noises she made and decided they were most encouraging when I licked up and down with short, quick flicks of my tongue. I don't know how long I was there. My jaw was aching. There was a danger my tongue would reach the point of muscle failure. Then her breathing grew deeper and faster. Her hands were round my head and she grabbed two fistfuls of my hair. Her body tensed. Her groin bucked against my face with a force which was almost frightening. She let out a satisfied grunt and her body went limp. Her hands released my hair and gently caressed my head. "Thank you, Peter," she said, quietly. I realized I'd successfully brought her to orgasm. I wanted to set off on a victory lap round the campus, shouting to everyone, "My name is Peter and I can make a woman cum!"

There was a lull. I lifted my head to look at Sophie's face. Her eyes were closed and she was grinning broadly, which made me feel good. I could not only make a woman cum: I could also make her happy. I wasn't sure if I should leave her in that contented place or do something else. I thought of asking her to flip over so I could work my way up the other side of her. I'd read a lot about the erotic power of the butt and hadn't explored Sophie's at all. I decided it wasn't where I needed to be. The moment had arrived—no more talking, no more foreplay. Another thing I'd found in my college welcome pack was a strip of three condoms. I'd assumed they'd still be intact and unused on graduation day, but I'd put them in my bedside drawer, just in case. I took one out and opened the packet, taking care not to damage the contents. As I fumbled with the condom, I wished I'd practiced by myself so I had a better idea of how to put one on. The first time I tried, it was inevitably inside out and refused to unroll along my shaft. I turned it round and tried to put it on again. My penis objected to being forced into a straitjacket and wilted. This threatened to be more embarrassing than the first time. Fortunately, Sophie had read my reactions during the foreplay well enough that she knew what to do. "Kiss my feet again," she said, and then added, "I hope they fucking stink."

I didn't need to go anywhere near her feet. I'd never heard her use such language before and that word in her voice hit me like an electric shock. More importantly, she'd shown me a hint of the kinkiness and meanness that I'd assumed only existed in the Sophie of my fantasies. If they existed in the real person as well, it promised untold excitements for the future. My cock immediately sprang back to its full size and the condom slid on easily. We were good to go.

I lay on top of Sophie and kissed her. I felt her pubes against mine so I knew I was in roughly the right place. I wasn't sure what was supposed to happen next. Did a penis lock on to its target and burrow in automatically? I soon realized this wasn't how it worked. I put my hand between Sophie's legs, found the entrance to her pussy, felt it with my middle finger, and placed the tip of my cock in the right place. By the time I was back in penetrating position, my cock had slipped and was nudging up against her vulva or perineum. It was good Sophie had more experience than I had. She took the base of my cock between two fingers and a thumb. I was glad I'd cum twice during the night. Without a process of desensitization, a naked woman touching my cock would have caused another unfortunate incident. When she had me in the right place, she said, "Now, push." I moved forward and penetrated her easily. Even through a condom, I could feel my penis engulfed in the most delicious soft warmth. I took a moment to appreciate that I was inside a woman. I didn't want to dwell on this too long. Although I'd achieved my primary objective when I made her cum, I wanted this to last as long as possible. I moved slowly inside her, enjoying the friction of her tight pussy around my cock. However much I wanted to focus on the sensation of the moment, my mind couldn't help but whisper in Sophie's ear, "What am I doing?"

She picked up on what I wanted to hear and said loudly, "You're fucking me, Peter."

As I should have known, this took me to the point of no return. I let it happen. I felt my cock contracting. I was cumming inside her. Even if sex with me was such a traumatic experience that Sophie never saw me again, I had taken an important step forward in life. I was definitely not a virgin anymore. By all conceivable measures, my cherry had been lost.

We naturally fell into a post-coital position of her lying on her back with my head resting on her breasts. For a while I simply enjoyed being sated while breathing in her scent, but I had to ask the classic question, "How was it for you?"

"It was nice," she said. Maybe not the word I was hoping for but I couldn't expect it to be awe-inspiring or earth-shattering the first time. "What about you?"

"It's the only thing I want to do for the rest of my life."

She kissed the top of my head and said, "You're silly."

SEVEN

MARK

IT SOMETIMES LOOKED LIKE PETER WAS trying to avoid me when he was with his girl, Sophie. He had introduced us and she'd smiled sweetly at me. She looked okay. The dark skin and black hair gave her an exotic look which I liked. She was obviously a geek, but as I've said before, I didn't mind. I knew she'd play computer games and know every frame of the *Lord of the Rings* movies. If she wanted me to dress up as a hobbit during sex, I wouldn't object, as long as she paid for the costume.

I had other things on my mind during my first few weeks at college. The intensity of soccer training was an eye-opener. I'd always taken the game seriously, but it was nothing like this before. Endless practice of set pieces, drilling shots on goal until it was impossible to aim the ball anywhere else. Long sessions of agility training, running, cycling, and lifting weights. Training was up to seven hours a day. I was then expected to show some sort of interest in academic work. I was so tired I almost—almost, that is!—had no energy left for women.

I was pleased to see a number of women training alongside the men. They had slim, toned bodies and, for reasons I didn't fully understand, most had blonde ponytails. Nothing wrong with that package, but I had my eye on something more challenging. One of our fitness trainers was a woman called Nicole, who was in her early thirties. She didn't know much about playing soccer, but knew everything about the human body and how to get it into shape. She worked us hard, but I liked her. I always got the feeling she wanted us to be as good as we could be. Whenever she wasn't talking about health and fitness, she was rhapsodizing about her new husband. They'd been married a month and, to hear her talk about him, you'd think he was the perfect combination of intellectual, saint, and fitness guru. She was in the first flush of married life and loved her husband more than anything. So, obviously, I had to fuck her.

This wasn't as difficult as you'd imagine. Because she was newly-married, she hadn't completely thrown off her single-girl mindset. She and her husband hadn't yet gotten into the groove of the couple who always do everything together. She still went out with her own friends. One day, I walked past her while she was talking on the phone. I heard her arranging to meet some friends in a nearby bar at eight in the evening. I don't know if Nicole meant me to hear that. On reflection, I think not. Just one of those happy coincidences. I saw my chance to spend time with her off duty. She'd never seen me in anything except a sweaty sports kit. Her first sight of me dressed for an evening out would blow her away.

I'd turned one wall of my room at the pad into a space to hang up my clothes. From this, I selected a perfectly pressed white shirt, midnight blue trousers, and an Oxford gray jacket. Dressed like this, I walked the twenty minutes to the bar Nicole had mentioned. I timed my arrival to be forty minutes after she'd met up with her friends. If I got there too early, she might not pay me any attention because she'd be too busy catching up. I wanted to give her time to get a little bored with her friends and be open for some distraction.

Walking into the bar, I was surprised. I'd expected Nicole to frequent a sports bar full of jocks shouting abuse at a widescreen

TV. In this place, two middle-aged couples were finishing a steak dinner at one end of the room. An old guy was enjoying a beer while he read the evening paper. It wasn't hard to spot Nicole, sitting at a table with two other women. I liked this arrangement. The other two could talk to each other if I separated Nicole from the pack. I didn't show any sign of having seen her as I walked past their table. I leaned against the bar but didn't do anything to attract the barman's attention. Even with my back to the room, I could sense Nicole's approach and knew to the second when I'd feel her hand on my arm. "Hey!" I said, putting on my best surprised but pleased face.

"What brings you here?" she asked.

"I was going to meet a friend but he's been delayed. I figured I might as well have a drink while I'm here."

"It would be a shame not to. Here, let me buy you one."

"You always tell us about the importance of being in peak condition at all times. Should you be encouraging me to drink?"

"Everyone's allowed a cheat day once in a while. If it makes you feel better, I'll get you to run ten more laps of the track for every drink you have."

"Sounds reasonable. I'll have a beer."

"Even for a cheat day, beer's too high in calories. You can have a gin and diet tonic." I didn't tell her I had a few beers even on non-cheat days. It didn't matter what I had to drink this evening. I'd only sip on it. This evening was not about being drunk. I wanted to be on top of my game. I had no intention of getting her drunk, either. That makes things too easy. I want a woman to be in complete command of her faculties when she gives herself to me. I have techniques that don't depend on alcohol. One insecurity a married woman often has is that no one will ever find her attractive again. Her husband tells her how beautiful she is, but he's under a contractual obligation. The trick is to compliment her, but be subtle. If you're too obvious in your attempt at seduction, loyalty to her husband might kick in and she'll back off. I looked her up and down, slowly and deliberately. She had clearly dressed for a night out with friends rather than for seduction in a simple white blouse, stonewashed jeans, and white trainers. "Do you want a photo?" she asked.

"I thought I was being so subtle."

"Something you need to work on."

When our drinks arrived, we sat at the bar with them. She showed no sign of wanting to go back to her friends. This was promising. "What's a young guy like you doing hanging out at this old timers' bar?" she asked me.

"More to the point, you could be with anyone you wanted, so why are you having a quiet drink with the girls?"

She tried to look affronted, but not before the half-second grin on her face showed how much she appreciated the compliment. "I'm a respectable married woman. What do you expect me to do?"

This started her off on that thing a wife sometimes does: mentioning her marital status in every sentence. "I was talking to Lucas, he's my husband, today, and he said . . . Ever since I got married, I've found out . . . Some of the other women in my building are youngish wives—like me—with husbands—like me—and they often . . .."

This didn't worry me. On the contrary, she was convincing herself far more than me that she was married and therefore unavailable. It meant she was bothered about how she felt when she was with me. I waited until she'd run out of ways to crowbar her husband into the conversation and then I said, "I so admire what you've done. A woman like you has so many options and you've cut yourself off from them deliberately. It's brave. I couldn't do it. To know you're going to touch the same person for the rest of your life. You must be so sure you've made the right choice."

"Oh . . . I'm sure," she said, in an unsure voice.

"You've found someone perfect."

"Well . . . nobody's perfect."

My hand was under the table so she didn't see me clenching my fist in triumph. She might as well have bent over the bar and let me fuck her there and then. From that point, it was inevitable we'd end up in bed together. "So what's not perfect about him?"

The first things she mentioned weren't important. He didn't always remember to turn on the extractor fan when he was in the shower. Sometimes, he forgot how she took her coffee and made it with one sugar too many. I listened sympathetically and asked questions that probed just enough. Soon, she was railing against her husband's habit of pretending to listen to her but keeping one eye on the TV. She couldn't stand the way he subtly patronized her brother because he worked in a factory. After half an hour, she was feeling something akin to dislike for her husband. Fortunately, she had a handsome, charming young man in front of her who could help her forget her marital woes if only for one night. "Lucas is away tonight," she said. "Can you walk me home? Our part of town isn't safe for a woman on her own." I wasn't a bit surprised to discover the area where they lived was perfectly nice with no hint of danger anywhere.

As soon as their front door closed behind us, I put my hands on her shoulders and moved my mouth toward hers. At first, she turned away, maybe thinking sex wasn't cheating so long as no kissing was involved. This didn't worry me particularly. My experience with Ashley had taught me it's perfectly possible to have great sex without any kissing. It turned out Nicole couldn't resist for long and soon our tongues were locked together. I spent longer on this part than I ordinarily would. I was pretty sure it was an important moment for her. For the first time in her married life, she was kissing a man other than her husband. She needed a moment to process this, but not long enough for her to decide it was wrong. I kept things moving quickly so there wouldn't be too much time for reflection. I unbuttoned her blouse and pushed it off her shoulders. I moved in to kiss her neck. I guess there must be some women in the world who don't like this, but I've never met any. Her hands were on my back and she was making feral little murmurs. I always enjoy this moment when a woman's education and sophisticated ways are stripped back to leave only her animal-istic core. I didn't so much remove her bra as grab it and shake her tits out of it. They were surprisingly big. When I saw her in train-ing, they were always strapped up and restrained inside a sports bra. They seemed to inflate as they fell free. I massaged the left one roughly with my strong fingers. Her murmurs became deeper and gruffer as a little pain mixed in with the pleasure. I didn't know my way around the house but I maneuvered her through the nearest door, hoping it wouldn't lead to a closet. I got lucky and found myself in the dining room. A big table dominated the center of the room. I tried to bend her over it, possibly to fuck her from behind but at least to get those jeans down and check out her ass. "No," she said, "if we're going to do this, let's go all the way." I'd been fully intending to go all the way, but I figured out quickly what she meant. Once again, my experience with Ashley stood me in good stead. It's a fundamental difference between men and women. If a man's cheating on his wife, he generally wants to do it in a hotel room where there's a team of cleaners who'll come in and destroy the evidence. He wants to minimize his chance of being caught. Women, on the other hand, often relish the added layer of infidelity that comes from having sex with another guy in the marital bed. It's where a husband and wife can make love and also rest securely, knowing this is their sacred space where no one can intrude. She then violates that space by bringing another man into it. "Follow me!" she said.

We went upstairs and through the first door on the right. It was the small but nice bedroom you'd expect a young couple to have. The double bed filled most of the space but there was room for wardrobes and bookcases on either side. She lay on the bed and extended her arms up to me. I would have liked her to take her clothes off first, but I could work around it. I took my jacket off and laid it on the bed, out of our way but within easy reach. I knew to lie beside her instead of on top of her. I kissed her while my fingers stroked her well-toned abs and explored the waistband of her jeans. She popped open the button and unzipped. My hand snaked in and found its way into her panties. My fingers curled around her vulva and the tip of my middle finger touched her clit. I rubbed it from side to side. She arched her back and her mouth opened wide. I watched her with something close to contempt. If I could get a reaction like that with a finger, imagine what I could do with my dick. I certainly didn't want to make her cum with my finger. That's a move reserved for a guy who has no faith in his cock. Nicole lifted her butt off the bed—a move I've always found sexy—to allow me to pull down her jeans and panties to her ankles. I didn't see any need to remove anything else. Her blouse was wide open and spread beneath her on the bed. Technically, she still had her bra on, but it was up in her armpits. Men are always told never to keep their socks on during sex, but I had no objection to Nicole leaving on both her socks and shoes. Her feet were not the most interesting part of her at that moment. I decided I wouldn't bother getting fully undressed either. If she wanted to put her hand inside my shirt to touch my chest I wouldn't stop her, but all I did was pull my trousers and shorts to my knees. It added to the feel of a quick and dirty fuck.

I took my wallet out of my jacket pocket. I found a condom and was about to open the packet, when she shook her head. "Too respectful," she said.

These words turned me on, but meant I couldn't enjoy the fuck as freely. I knew I had enough control to pull out at the right time, but it was an extra thing to keep in mind.

Everything we'd done so far had taken her a long way down the road of cheating on her husband. If Lucas had walked in at any point since we'd arrived back at their place, she'd have had trouble convincing him we were nothing more than friends. Nonetheless, the look on her face when I entered her had surprise in it, as well as pleasure. Here she was, a newly-married woman. She might have expected to feel the itch after a few years, but not after a few weeks. Her actions were at odds with her idea of what she should be doing, but she didn't stop me. On the contrary, she lay back and enjoyed every second of it. I got a good rhythm going as I thrust into her. Her breathing quickened and deepened. Her cunt was pulsating round my cock. She lifted her ass off the bed again and shouted, "Bastard!" as she came. Whether she meant me or her husband, or whether she was shouting randomly at the world, I didn't ask.

I would have liked to keep going until I came. With the lack of a condom closing that option to me, I rolled off and lay next to her. This was when the guilt could have kicked in. With the post-cumming dropping off of hormones, the reality of what she'd done might have come crashing in on her. There was no sign of that as she said, "Your turn." I hoped this was her cue to wrap her lips—the ones on her mouth, I mean—around my cock. Instead, she took it in her hand and pulled it. There was no reason to delay matters any further, so I focused on her tits and soon felt myself cumming. She cupped her hands around the end of my cock and I pumped my sperm into them. I wanted to pause long enough to enjoy the moment but she was already worrying about the clean-up process. Despite Nicole wanting to cheat on her husband in their bed, she didn't share Ashley's fetish for leaving traces of infidelity all over her home. She tipped the contents of her right hand into her left and took a Kleenex from her bedside table. Before she wiped my cum out of her left hand, she looked down and said, "Oh!" She'd seen her wedding ring, symbol of the bond she shared with her husband, covered in another man's seed. This was another moment when she could be suddenly overcome with remorse. This might manifest itself as hatred against the source: me. "I'd better go," I said, reaching down to pull up my jeans.

She put a hand on my arm. "No, don't go," she said quietly. "You came on my wedding ring."

"Right," I said, in a voice without expression.

"You have no respect for me, my husband, or my marriage." Talk like this might lead to a violent outburst against me. The sensible part of me said it was time to get out of the house with a minimum of fuss and act like nothing had happened next time I saw Nicole at training. Even though I'd just cum, the horny and curious parts of me got the better of the sensible part. Nicole got out of bed and walked quickly into the living room. I didn't know what I was supposed to do so stayed in bed, relaxed but alert. There was a possibility she'd come back with a gelding knife, intent on making me no further threat to her marriage. What she was actually carrying on her return was an album bound in red leather. "I want you to see this," she said, getting back onto the bed. We sat up in bed together like we were reading the Sunday papers and she opened the album. On the first page was a photo of Nicole, a solo one of her posing in her wedding dress. I was more used to seeing her in t-shirt and sweat pants. "How did I look on my wedding day?" she asked.

Her body was in such good shape it was hard to imagine anything not suiting her, but this was not what she wanted to hear. "You looked uncomfortable."

"Did I look stupid?"

"Yes, you looked fucking stupid." She moaned softly and turned the page to a picture of Lucas with his best man. Lucas was a runner who reckoned the time he spent pounding the track was exercise enough so he never went to the gym. His body was a straight line so his suit didn't so much hang on him as drip off him. There was more conviction in my voice as I said, "What a skinny little wimp."

She put her hand on my right bicep and I flexed it for her. "You could take him, couldn't you?"

"Easily," I replied, "and you'd enjoy seeing it."

She wasn't ready to commit to wanting her husband beaten up, but she said, "Show me what you think." It was a professionally produced album, which looked expensive, so I guessed she didn't want me to rip it. I puckered my lips and spat on the photo. It caught her husband full in the face, but his smile didn't waver. "I cannot believe you did that," she said. "You asshole." I didn't focus on her words so much as the growl of dark desire in her voice.

She flipped through the album, past all the photos of grinning
friends and relatives, to the final page showing Nicole and Lucas
kissing on their wedding day. "What do you think of that one?" I
didn't reply. Cum was leaking out of my cock. I rested the album
on my balls and wiped my cock across the photo, leaving a smear.
The record of their first kiss as a married couple was permanently
tainted with the seed of the wife's infidelity. She took the album
from me and placed it beside the bed. I wondered if she'd tell her
husband she'd been looking through it, reminiscing about their
special day. "Close your eyes," she said. Given how recently she'd
called me an asshole, it wasn't a good idea to close my eyes, but
I did it anyway. I heard drawers opening and closing, along with
a rustle of what sounded like tissue paper. After five minutes, she
said, "Open them." She was standing at the end of the bed, dressed
in matching white underwear. The floral pattern on the cups of her
bra hinted at nipples underneath without being too explicit. The
pattern was repeated in the tanga panties, lending an air of mys-
tery to her pussy. The casual observer wouldn't have known if she
was shaved, Brazilian, or landing strip. I already knew and wished
she'd worn this outfit at the start of the encounter. The outfit was
completed by white silk stockings with suspender belt. "This is my
wedding night lingerie," she said. It was the perfect combination of
sexy and demure for a blushing bride. Getting back into bed, she
added, "No one except my husband should ever see me in this, but
now I'm wearing it for you."

"Because you're a cheating slut," I told her.

"Because I'm a cheating slut," she confirmed. "What happens to
cheating sluts?"

"They get fucked."

I was hard for her again. She was so turned on by me violating
the symbols of her marriage that she didn't need any foreplay. I
went to pull down her panties, but she shook her head. "Push them
aside." Women are often convinced this is a trashy, sexy thing to
do, but for the man, it's uncomfortable and annoying having this

piece of cloth persistently digging into the base of his cock. I did what she said and started fucking her, but her panties were giving me a friction burn. I pulled out and grabbed the gusset, hoping she'd enjoy the dramatic gesture of her panties being roughly pulled off. Unfortunately, she mistimed lifting her butt off the bed and there was a sound of ripping fabric. "Shit!" she said. Her look changed from enjoying the wrongness of the situation to genuine worry about destroying something special to her and her husband. I tried to take her mind off it by putting my dick back inside her and fucking her hard. It worked, at least in the short term. I'm fairly sure she wasn't thinking about anything else as she came on my cock. Something told me I'd better not do any more damage to her property so I pulled out of her cunt. I shuffled up the bed until I was level with her head. I put my cock into her mouth. She sucked it for a couple of minutes and I came. She swallowed it all, so that was one thing at least she didn't have to worry about cleaning up. I got off the bed and she immediately held up the torn panties. She eyed them glumly for a moment then shrugged. "If Lucas asks, I'll remind him he ripped them by being so passionate on our wedding night."

No man in the world would argue with that, even if he didn't remember it. I left their place shortly afterwards, knowing I wouldn't be back.

EIGHT

PETER

SOPHIE AND I GOT INTO A routine. We would agree when she'd come to the pad for tea. It was always for tea because, of course, sex was the farthest thing from our minds. We'd sit in the den, drink tea, and talk for a while. Sophie and I never ran out of things to say to each other. I've heard of couples who use up all their stories in the first week and are bored ever after unless they take their clothes off. If Sophie and I had been taking different modules, we discussed those and made jokes about our professors and fellow students. I didn't need to fear the friend zone anymore, so we could happily discuss books, music, TV shows, and movies. I know everyone in a relationship is honor-bound to say their partner is also their best friend, but, in our case, it was the truth. Much as I liked talking to Mark, I preferred my chats with Sophie. After we'd finished the tea, we were like: I suppose, if you're not doing anything, if you have time, we could always . . . have a little bit of sex.

In my bedroom, we took our clothes off. There was nothing mysterious about our bodies anymore, so there was no teasing in the disrobing. We undressed quickly and got into bed. We normally spent a lot of time kissing. I'd always envied people who had someone to kiss and I wasn't going to take it for granted. To taste another person's mouth was so intimate. Sophie liked having her nipples sucked, so I did that, being careful not to favor one over the other. Moving away from them reluctantly, I slid under the quilt as Sophie parted her legs. I licked her and made her cum. As I got more experienced and understood better what worked for her, this process got faster and faster. I still don't know if this was a good thing or not. One advantage women have over men is no one minds if they cum too fast. It's not like I always stopped after her first orgasm. I kept going until she put her hands on my head and said, "Okay, babe." One time, she came three times while my head was between her legs. Maybe she was testing my endurance, but she certainly looked happy by the end of it.

After I'd made sure she was satisfied, I could have my fun. Usually, being in bed with her was enough to make me hard. Occasionally, though, my cock decided it wasn't needed during cunnilingus and stood down. When this happened, one or two caresses from Sophie's soft hand normally brought it back to life. If this didn't work, we discovered something else that did the trick. "It's so small," she said. "Such a limp little dick." On one occasion, she even added, "I've had bigger." I was shocked by how profoundly this turned me on. I didn't think anything could excite me more than having sex with a real woman, but I was affected at an even more visceral level by being compared to someone else—especially being compared unfavorably.

We tried different positions. Neither of us had much experience to draw on. Our go-to position was missionary, but I also enjoyed fucking her from behind. For a thin girl, her butt had a pleasing roundness to it. I loved gazing at it and grabbing hold of it during sex. I wasn't such a big fan of the cowgirl. Her breasts were too small to bounce but I enjoyed watching them wobble as she rode my cock. The thing I didn't like was my lack of control. In other positions, I could slow down if I felt myself about to cum. I found this slight delay led to a more intense orgasm. Sophie simply moved at a steady pace until I writhed under her and she knew I'd cum. Although *she* was happy to suggest improvements during sex, I was afraid of appearing ungrateful if I did the same so I acted as if every time was the last word in ecstasy.

One of the things I enjoyed most about the start of my relationship with Sophie was lying in bed together naked. Even when we weren't fucking, the air was thick with sex. The mixture of scents from Sophie's hair, breath, armpits, pussy, and feet created a literal hot bed of sensuality. Sometimes, we dozed or went out to get snacks, refueling for the next bout of sex. Sophie's capacity for being fucked appeared limitless so often we were waiting for me to be ready again. Even when I was in my twenties, my body needed some time to recover. During these times, we talked, not exclusively about sex, but it was a topic that kept coming up.

On one of these occasions, my mind was buzzing about Sophie comparing me to another man. It was mean of her to do it. I was darkly fascinated by her meanness and wanted to explore that side of her. I spent some time wondering if I should say anything. It was early enough in the relationship that I still had the fear she'd decide I wasn't the one if I said the wrong thing. The safe bet would have been to lie there, telling her how beautiful she was and how I adored everything about her. I decided to gamble. I could lose a lot or get something I was sure at that moment I wanted. I looked at her with a smile, hoping I could work my usual trick of passing it off as a joke if she reacted badly. "Sophie," I began. "You remember the first couple of times we were . . . fooling around?"

She laughed. "Is that what we're calling it? Yes, I vaguely remember a bit of fooling around."

"You'll also remember things finished . . . prematurely."

The sweet part of her nature came to the fore and she misinterpreted what I was saying. She gathered me into her bosom again, which was nice, so I wasn't complaining. "I told you, baby, it's not a problem. I've read about this. It happens a lot to guys when they're starting down this road. It's already so much better."

This was good to hear. It would have been sensible to let the matter drop there, but guys are famously low on sense when they're turned on. I raised my head. "That's so nice of you, Sophie. I was wondering if occasionally you could be . . . a little less nice?"

She frowned. "What do you mean?"

"You've probably always dreamed of a big strong alpha male."

"Most of the time I dreamed of meeting someone who gets me."

This would have been another good moment for me to shut up but I carried on, "But you want someone powerful and assertive in bed, not a guy who loses control at the sight of a semi-naked woman."

Understanding was dawning in her face. "Mm . . . okay."

"So . . . what did you really think about what happened?"

"You came in your shorts because you couldn't control yourself around a breast. You were . . . a twat."

An electric thrill ran through me. It wasn't the word I'd have chosen, but it was the rudest thing I'd ever heard her say about anyone. I didn't want her to lose her essential Sophie niceness, but I wanted to know this other side of her. I finally accepted it was unwise to pursue it any further at that moment. I let it go and kissed her.

Another time, we were in bed together. Sophie kissed her way down my hairless chest and over the slight bulge of my belly. As I felt her hot breath on my erect cock, I realized it was going to be another first for me. I was afraid the sight of my cock disappearing into a woman's mouth would lead to another embarrassing incident. Even so, it wasn't something I could miss and I lifted my head so I could see. It was a powerful image but, to be honest, I was disappointed by the feeling. I was in a warm and soft place, but there wasn't much friction. It was like soaking in a hot bath, pleasant and comforting but not particularly sexy. She moved her mouth away from my cock and looked me in the eye. "Don't cum in my mouth, Peter. Daniel did that with me once. It's the only thing he did which grossed me out. I do not like the taste."

As soon as she said I couldn't cum in her mouth, it became something I badly wanted to do. Still, I wanted a whole lot more for Sophie to keep returning to my bed so didn't want it associated with anything she found gross. After five minutes, I gently removed my cock from her mouth and returned the compliment by licking her. I had no objection to *her* cumming in *my* mouth, so I kept going until she did. I put on a condom and fucked her. Now she'd told me I was getting better, my confidence was increasing. I was able to keep my thrusts going for longer before I had to pause to let my excitement subside. I always took a sneaky look at the bedside clock at the start and finish. I was getting up around the ten-minute mark from penetration to ejaculation.

Her thoughts often turned to food after sex. She'd told me she liked peaches, so I'd bought a bag of them. It was a healthier post-coital snack than chocolate and potato chips. As she nibbled on one of the peaches, I lay beside her, idly stroking her belly and thighs. It still struck me as strange and wonderful that I had access to a female body. She finished her peach, put the stone on the bedside table, and lay on the bed. Stretching sensually like a cat in the sun, she said, "That feels nice. You have the magic touch, Peter." This was good to hear. As her hands went behind her head and her fingers touched the back wall, Sophie's armpits were revealed in all their hirsute glory. Every encounter with them made me love them more. I liked the hairs tickling my nose as I kissed them. She'd lain off the deodorant and the musky, raw onion scent of her pits bypassed my brain and hit me straight in a primal part of myself. I kissed and licked her left armpit, appreciating the different notes of acid and salt. I was discovering that Sophie's armpits, if left to mellow naturally, had a taste almost as complex as the one emanating from between her legs. I don't know how much pleasure Sophie derived from this, but my fascination intrigued her. "You like my armpits, don't you?"

"Yes, I do. I'm not sure why."

"Have you considered the possibility you're a pervert?"

"You bring out the pervert in me."

"At least I help you achieve your full potential."

"Does anyone know about your hairy armpits?" I asked.

I couldn't help bringing other people into our pillow talk. It sometimes made Sophie roll her eyes. On this occasion, she was silent for a moment. "I'm trying to remember if I shaved before I went to the beach the last time. I didn't realize my armpits were of such vital importance until I met you so I didn't keep a journal of when they were smooth or hairy. I suppose my doctor might have seen them, but no real reason why he should have. I haven't been to him with any armpit-related illnesses."

"So this is something only the two of us know."

"I suppose so. Why?"

"It's a secret between us. I know something about you that's hidden from the rest of the world."

"Yes, everyone else looks at me and sees sweet and pure. Only you know I have sweaty, hairy, stinky armpits." She put her hand on my cock and smiled as she felt how hard I was. "You definitely are a pervert."

I definitely was. The close proximity of her armpits coupled with her words about them had my heart pounding and my cock straining. I had a strong desire to fuck her, but knew I might finish too quickly. Instead, I continued stroking her. My hand found its way to her bush. Parting the hairs, I put my finger on her clit and rubbed it gently from side to side. She moaned softly. I knew she wanted to have sex, but I decided to delay a little longer. There was something else I wanted to talk about. "Sophie," I began, quietly.

"Mm?" she responded, her eyes still closed as my finger rubbed her.

"What do you call this thing I'm touching now?"

"You mean my clit?"

"No, I mean the whole area I'm focusing on."

She opened her eyes and gave me a mischievous look. "I could call it my vaginal region," she said.

"You could," I agreed. "Is that what you call it?"

She bit her lip like she couldn't believe how bad she was being. "No, I call it my cunt."

This made me tremble with desire. I'd dared to hope she might use the word 'pussy,' so 'cunt' was beyond anything I'd hoped for. My cock had never been so big or so hard. It bobbed between us, desperate to be satisfied. Sophie's cunt—I could use the word with impunity now—was getting wetter. I lay on top of her. I was more worried than ever about cumming too quickly and I wanted to be at maximum arousal until I was sure she'd finished talking. I penetrated Sophie but didn't dare move except to kiss her. "What do you call this thing you've got inside you?" I asked.

"Your dick . . . your cock." She vacillated, trying to decide which word was ruder.

I wasn't sure either, but I made a decision. "It's my cock," I told her.

"I've got your cock inside my cunt." I already knew this, but it was still good to hear it from her. My shy, nerdy girlfriend was using all these crude words and I loved her all the more for it.

I wasn't finished yet. Supporting myself on my elbows, I put my hands on her chest and massaged the small but perfect orbs. "What are these?" I asked.

"My breasts," she said.

I don't know if she was deliberately teasing, but it sounded a bit too biology textbook for me. "No, they're your tits."

"My tits," she said, meditatively, like she'd never thought of herself as having tits before.

"I love your tits," I told her, squeezing them a bit harder.

She felt she had to say something complimentary in return so she said, "I love your cock."

I never expected to hear a real-life female saying anything like this about my genitalia. "What do you want me to do with my cock?" I asked her.

"What we're already doing. I want to make love." This was good, but she realized it wasn't what I wanted to hear. She whispered in my ear, "Fuck me, Peter."

Once again, this was a word too far. I felt I was about to cum. In the excitement of everything we were doing and saying, I'd forgotten to put on a condom. "Where do you want me to cum?" I asked her, urgently, as I pulled out.

"How about on my ass?" she said.

It was one part of her we hadn't officially named yet. It aroused me too much. Much as I would have loved to cum over her ass, I didn't manage to hold it and came over her thigh. "Sorry," I said.

"It's okay, baby," she said.

"Don't be nice," I said, in a strangled voice.

"You fucking loser," she said. I'd just cum so these words didn't excite me at that moment, but I banked them in my memory, knowing I'd be thinking about them for the rest of my life.

NINE

SOPHIE

DO YOU THINK I COULD SAY something now?

I remember the first time I met Peter, back at the party when we were both sixteen. I realized how timid around girls he was from the way he sat next to me. Most guys would have taken the opportunity to touch or at least brush against a girl. He kept six inches between us at all times. I knew I could use his shyness. I thought of asking him to get me a Coke . . . well, *telling* him with no please or thank you. I knew he'd do it. It wouldn't occur to him to refuse a woman's demand. I wasn't exactly loaded with confidence myself back then so I didn't tell him, but I thought about it afterwards. Not the most salacious fantasy ever, but I found it strangely arousing.

When I met Peter again at college, I saw he was still nervous. I was feeling lost in the new environment too. What I needed was a friend. It outweighed any desires I had about power plays—although I still had those thoughts. When we became more than friends, it was interesting to watch Peter grope toward what he wanted. I was keen to help him find his way, but it had to come from him. If I'd told Peter to smear his naked body in honey and kick a hornets' nest, he'd have done it, but he needed to tap into *his* desires, not just mine.

One afternoon, we were lying in bed in my college room. I was lucky—or unlucky, however you look at it—in having a room to myself. I occasionally envied the camaraderie of those who were sharing, but at least I didn't have to wait in line for the bathroom. Peter gulped a couple of times, a sure sign he was about to say something controversial. "You remember the other day?"

"You'll have to be a bit more specific."

He gulped again. "I was remembering in particular the part when I was licking you and you were telling me what to do. I kind of liked it."

"The licking or the telling?"

"I meant the telling. Obviously, I liked the licking."

"You liked having a woman tell you what to do?" He nodded. "Aren't men supposed to be the dominant ones, ordering around the weak and submissive women?"

"I'm not like other men."

"Ain't that the truth!" I said. I laughed while I said it, but I felt something moving inside me. I have no illusions about myself as a great beauty. The best I can say about myself is I'm cute. As a result, I've not always had my choice of men. For this reason, I tend to be a people pleaser. If I can't get by on my looks, I have to fall back on the consolation prize of a nice personality. I smile and try to be helpful. If anyone makes a comment suggesting I might be a nerd or a geek, I laugh along and show what a good sport I am. Peter's words made me realize I had real power over a man for the first time. The Sophie who'd had those teenage fantasies about telling Peter what to do reared her head again. "All right then, Peter, go and clean the basin in my bathroom. The cleaning products are in the cabinet."

This wasn't what Peter had in mind. He'd have preferred to stay in bed and have me order him to service me sexually. Even so, his dick was hard as he got out of bed and went into my bathroom. I stayed in bed, enjoying the snacks Peter had brought. If I'm honest, I touched myself a little too. I liked this new twist in our relationship and I was looking forward to seeing where it would take us.

After ten minutes, he came back into the bedroom, still erect. "I think it's okay. Do you want to have a look?"

I hopped out of bed and went into the bathroom, doing my best impression of a sergeant inspecting the barracks. At first sight, it looked like Peter had done a good job. The bowl was spotless white and the tap was sparkling in the ceiling light. Then I noticed a little patch of black scum lurking under the tap. "What's that?" I said, sharply. His eyes widened as he looked at it, so he didn't deliberately do a bad job to see how I'd react. He sprayed the offending area with cleaning fluid and went at it vigorously with the scourer. After he'd finished, it was perfectly clean, but we knew he hadn't completed his task to my satisfaction. We didn't say anything. We both instinctively knew what would happen next. He stood in the middle of the bathroom and, showing impressive flexibility, bent over and grasped his own ankles. Peter's skinny bottom was looking up at me. If I was going to do this, I was going to do it full-blooded. I stood behind him, sideways on. I raised my hand above my head and brought it down as hard as I could on Peter's right buttock. I'm not the strongest person in the world but there was a satisfying crack as my hand landed. He cried out. There was a wicked throb in my stomach as I saw the white skin of his buttock turn pink. I took half a step back and smacked his left buttock, trying to make it even harder if I could. He straightened up and turned to face me. I'd never seen his cock so big. "Bed! Now!" I said. We went back into the bedroom. What we'd already done was more than enough foreplay. I was as wet as he was hard. He lay on top of me and I put him inside me. Looking up at his face, I recognized his frown. It was more than the look of concentration he had while inside me. He was debating whether he should say something or not. "What's on your mind, Peter?" I asked him.

"You spanked me," he said, in a strangled voice.

"You noticed, did you?" I replied.

"It hurt," he continued.

"That's kind of the point with spanking."

"You wanted to hurt me."

"Yes, Peter. I spanked you and I did it as hard as I could because I wanted it to hurt."

"Sophie, I want . . . ." He trailed off, too embarrassed to say what was on his mind.

I gave him a reassuring kiss. "Peter, it's me, Sophie, your girl-friend. I . . . ." I stopped myself, realizing I was on the point of telling Peter I loved him for the first time. It wasn't the moment for that. "You can tell me anything."

It came out in a rush. "I want you to do that again, soon, and I want you to do that a lot."

TEN

PETER

I SOMETIMES WONDER HOW DIFFERENT MY LIFE would have been if I'd simply shut up when I was in bed with Sophie. I haven't talked much to others about their sex lives. The snippets I have heard suggest that, for a lot of people, sex is pretty much a silent activity. If there is any talking, it tends to be little more than, "Ow, can you move your elbow, babe? It's sticking into my ribs." I asked so many questions because I was curious. I found sex deeply fascinating and wanted to know everything about it. Sophie had a little more experience than me. Every time I began a new line of inquiry, I had fear Sophie would snap at me, something along the lines of, "For heaven's sake, Peter, could I come to bed once in a while without facing an interrogation?"

Despite this, I couldn't help myself. Another time, as we were lying in bed, I asked her, "You remember you told me about the guy you had a thing with last summer?"

Far from getting annoyed, she looked almost sheepish, as if she'd done something wrong. "Daniel, you mean? It was a fling, babe. He meant nothing. Well, maybe not nothing, but it didn't compare with what we have."

It was nice of her to offer reassurance, but it wasn't what I wasn't looking for. "You said he was an older guy."

"It's not like he tottered about on his walking frame. He was only about five years older than us."

"I guess you weren't his first."

"We didn't talk too much," she said. "Some people like to get on with it," she added, with a subtle dig. "But, no, I definitely wasn't his first."

"So . . . was he good?"

"I don't want to offend you, Peter," she said.

"The truth is the truth," I reminded her.

"Yes, it is. The truth is, he knew what he was doing. I'm glad I was with someone experienced. He made sure my first time was a good time, something to be repeated. If he'd been no good, I might not have wanted to do it again and we wouldn't be here now. In a way, you should thank him."

"If I ever meet him, I will." I made light of it, but the idea of thanking another man for fucking my girlfriend was exciting. Unable to quit while I was ahead, I asked, "Was he bigger than me?"

"Lengthways, only about two inches." Only? For an extra two inches, I'd have paid the price of a small car. She was learning that a matter-of-fact tone turned me on more than trying to be sensationalist. "He was a lot thicker, though," she said.

"He stretched you?" I asked.

"More like he filled me."

"How long did he last?"

"Let's just say Daniel had learned to control himself a bit better."

"How long, Sophie?"

"Anything between half an hour and an hour. One time, he kept going for an hour and a half. I was sore by the end, but it was so hot to be fucked long and hard."

"He sounds much better than me."

I assumed this was just pillow talk banter to turn us both on before we had sex, but Sophie looked straight at me and her tone changed in a way that immediately made me uneasy. "Yes, Peter, he was. Listen, I like the way you use your tongue on me. I really do. It feels nice, but it's not what I need. I didn't feel for Daniel even one per cent of what I feel for you, but there's one thing I miss about him. He fucked me until I came. I didn't think it was important, but every time you lick me to orgasm, I'm reminded of how Daniel made me cum with his cock. I need to feel it again. Will you ever be able to do that for me, Peter?"

I thought I liked being unfavorably compared to others. Faced with this sort of pressure, though, my cock had crumpled in on itself. I lay on the bed, thinking if I couldn't satisfy Sophie the way she wanted, she'd find someone who could. I was cursing myself for mentioning Daniel. Why hadn't I kept quiet and fucked her?

SOPHIE

AFTER THAT, PETER TRIED SO HARD. He wore three condoms in the hope it would desensitize his cock and make him last longer. It added a nice extra bit of girth, but didn't help with his staying power. Another time, he penetrated me and I could see he was trying desperately to think about something else. His eyes were screwed up in concentration like he was doing the thirty seven times table in his head. There was a danger I'd laugh, so I slowed things down by gently pushing him out of me and rolling onto my front. "What are you doing?" he asked.

"Mixing things up a bit," I said, mysteriously.

He adapted quickly to the new terrain, kissing my shoulders and down my back. He did his usual trick of skipping over my middle section and descending my legs. It felt nice when he kissed the back of my thighs. "I wish you could grow hair in the backs of your knees," he said, which was weird, but not a complete surprise.

"Ew," was all I could say to that.

If you're lying naked on your front, though, there's only going to be one primary focus. I felt Peter's hot breath on my ass, followed by the first of many kisses. I could tell he was nervous about opening the drapes. His thumbs found their way into my crack, then lost their nerve, and went back to massaging my buttocks. Finally, curiosity won out and he spread my cheeks. While I congratulated myself on not farting, he paused nervously. "Do it," I said, quietly.

He decided it was like going for a swim in icy water. The only way to do it was to dive straight in. His tongue probed my tight little asshole, going as deep as possible. I'd had a shower recently so I was fairly confident all was squeaky clean down there, but you can never be sure with assholes. I also had a feeling of power. People say, "Kiss my ass!" to assert their superiority over another person. Now I had someone doing it for real. Peter was so much in love with me—or, at least, in lust with my body—that he was excited by even the grossest part of me. He licked me for about ten minutes before raising his head. "How does my tongue feel in your asshole?" he asked.

"So good," I said, without a word of a lie.

"Do you . . . er . . . want me to put anything else in there?" he asked with a mixture of hope and nervousness.

"No, you're okay. Come up here and talk to me." He started moving up the bed but I pointed to the basin. "Mouthwash before you kiss me, Peter." When his breath was more minty and less buttholy, I said, "That was nice. I'd like you to do it again some time, but I've never wanted to have anal sex. Why would you want to do it anyway? There's a much nicer hole next door. It feels good for you and good for me when you put your cock inside it. Why don't you just fuck my cunt right now?"

He wasn't about to say no.

ELEVEN

PETER

ON THE NOTICE BOARD OUTSIDE THE dining hall was a big poster announcing, 'Saturday night—dance your way back to the 1970s.' Before, I wouldn't have dreamed of going to something like that. I'd have seen it as yet another opportunity to stand at the back of a room and be ignored. It was good to think, "I might go! With my girlfriend!"

Sophie liked the idea. I doubt she'd have gone on her own, either. We were both discovering the perks of being in a couple. We set about deciding what we'd wear to the dance. Our first notion was to go as a couple of disco divas. The only trouble was we didn't have luminous white suits or anything in gold lamé. As impoverished students, we couldn't splash out on costumes we'd only wear once. If we didn't have enough money to be glamorous, we could certainly afford the distressed look. We decided to go as punks. I had an old pair of jeans, already through in the knees. We took scissors to it until it was nothing more than a series of holes connected by strands of denim. A visit to the thrift shop furnished us with a black t-shirt, a short tartan skirt, and a pair of black stockings. On Saturday evening, Sophie and I went to our own rooms to get ready. She was going to call for me at eight. It didn't take me long to get ready. I sacrificed a white t-shirt by writing 'ANARCHY' across it with a black marker pen. I put this on with my ripped jeans and used gel to spike up my hair. It was only ten past seven so I worked on an assignment—not a very punk thing to do—until there was a knock at the door. I gasped when I saw Sophie. My quiet, nerdy girlfriend had transformed herself. Her hair was up in a Mohican. She was wearing black lipstick and eye shadow. Tribal markings were painted all over her face and neck in makeup. She'd attached safety pins to her earrings and used more safety pins to hold together some of the bigger holes in her black t-shirt and tartan skirt. Her stockings were also ripped and she was wearing a pair of big, black boots, which I'd never seen on her before. "Wow," I said, "you look great." Part of me wanted to forget about the dance and fuck this punk goddess in front of me. Maybe she picked up on that because she didn't come into the room. She grabbed my arm and said, "Hey, ho, let's go," which was a very punk thing to say.

The hall was full by the time we arrived. There were other punks. Some people had managed to go full disco. Others weren't dressed as anything in particular but wore flared trousers and brightly colored shirts. Then there were those who hadn't made an effort and were in their normal clothes. I felt superior to them. A few cabaret style tables had been set up next to the dance floor. Sophie saw a free one and immediately sat down. "This might be our only chance," she said. I didn't know why she was so keen to sit at a dance but I left her there while I went to the bar to get two glasses of wine. Sitting there with our drinks, we weren't sure what to do. We couldn't talk because the music was too loud. We didn't dance because Sophie was worried about losing our table. We people-watched and listened to the music. It was a mix of Abba, the Bee Gees, Rod Stewart, and such like. When the Clash's 'London Calling' came on, people took to the dancefloor to pogo. A guy came up to our table. He'd gone full Sid Vicious with an unfastened leather jacket over his bare chest and a padlock round his neck. The difference was Sid had a drug addict's wasted body. This guy looked like he knew the inside of a gym. He didn't seem to notice me and asked Sophie, "Care to join me in a grapple?"

I thought she'd at least glance in my direction to see if I minded her dancing with someone else. Without looking at me, she said, "Don't let anyone take my seat." They walked onto the dance floor. Sophie had never pogoed before. I doubt he had either. They jumped up and down in front of each other, looking a bit silly. The song ended and there was a jarring transition to Eric Clapton's 'Wonderful Tonight.' No one has ever pogoed to that song, so I expected Sophie to come back to the table. Instead, the guy put his arms around her shoulders for a slow dance. This was her opportunity to say, "Sir, you strangely forget yourself. I am here with my boyfriend." Instead, she put her arms around his waist. My girlfriend was dancing closely entwined with another guy. I had an urge to rush over and break it up, but two things stopped me. He was bigger than me. More importantly, I wasn't sure how Sophie would react. She'd put her arms around him voluntarily. It wasn't like he was forcing her into anything. I'd heard other women complaining about their boyfriends, saying things like, "He gets so jealous," or, "He's such a possessive jerk." I did not want to be that guy. I couldn't believe how close they were to each other. Her breasts—albeit protected by a t-shirt and bra— were brushing against his naked chest. Despite my efforts to be cool, I was jealous and embarrassed. Quite a few people knew Sophie and I were together. What would they think if they saw her with someone else?

Then I realized: my heart was pounding; my breathing was ragged; my cock was rock hard. Sophie wasn't the world's leading expert at flirting but she held his gaze, smiling at him shyly, and moving sensuously against him. I didn't know to what extent she was doing it out of attraction for him and how much was putting on a show for me. As the dance went on, my excitement was tempered with uneasiness. What guarantee did I have she'd come back to me afterwards? We'd only been dating a few weeks. It's not like I had much hold over her. Was he her boyfriend now? I was relieved when the song finished and she came back to our table. Maybe she was feeling guilty because she shouted in my ear, "We're not dancers. Do you want to go?"

I didn't hesitate. I wanted to be alone with her. We went back to my room. Mark's door was shut. I didn't know if he was in his room or out, but I was glad he wasn't around, wanting to talk to us. Sophie and I both knew we weren't there for a cup of tea. We went straight into my room and closed the door behind us. Lying next to her on my bed, I was glad she didn't act coy and say, "What? I didn't do anything. We were only dancing." Instead, she asked me, "Did you like watching me dance with that guy, Peter?"

"I was jealous."

"But did you enjoy it?" She put her hand on my bulge. She smiled as she felt how hard I was. "That answers that question."

"Did *you* enjoy it?" I asked.

"What, dancing with him?"

"Making me jealous."

She took a moment to think about it instead of telling me what I wanted to hear. "Yes, I did." I would have liked to talk more about this, but she changed the subject. "How do I look as a punkette?"

"Great, but it seems a bit of a waste. We spent a lot of time getting ourselves into seventies garb and didn't even stay there half an hour."

"I didn't dress up for them. It was for you. I thought you might like having a punky girlfriend. A real wild child. Your parents would not like me."

"They'd be appalled if they saw me with you. So . . . what do punk girlfriends do?"

"I do know a little about this. My brother's into punk and he's shown me a few documentaries about the scene. I know punks swear a lot."

My heart beat more quickly at this. Some people object to women swearing, saying it's unladylike, but I've always liked it. "Does punk Sophie swear a lot?"

"Yes, she fucking does," said Sophie, defiantly. "She's a . . . fucking foul-mouthed . . . fucking bitch . . . cunt." She looked at me and laughed. "I'm not good at this."

"I beg to differ," I said. "What does punk Sophie like the most?"

There was a danger she'd reply, "Peaches," but she knew what I wanted to hear. "Punk Sophie likes having a big cock inside her wet cunt and she likes being fucked like the nasty girl she is."

"*My* big cock?" I had to ask.

"Not necessarily."

I loved hearing her talk like this, but she was finding it difficult. I gave her a way out by asking, "What does punk Sophie want to do now?"

I assumed she'd say, "Punk Sophie wants to get fucked." Instead, she bit her lip and said, "There was a punk group called the Damned who sang about smashing things up."

I wasn't sure where she was going with this. "Right . . .?"

"Mindless destruction is just . . . wrong."

It was another thing I'd never thought about. It was a bizarre thing to do, a long way removed from traditional sexual activities. For some reason I couldn't explain, my cock pulsed inside my jeans at the idea of my punk girlfriend doing something so wanton. "You want to smash up some of my things?"

"Yes, Peter, I do." We looked around the room. Despite my state of arousal, I was level-headed enough to know I didn't want her smashing things my parents had given me or anything I needed for life at college. "Where's your porn?" she asked.

Blushing, I stammered, "Well . . . I . . . you're all I need . . .."

"Come on, Peter. I may not know too much about men, but even I know every boy keeps a couple of magazines under his bed to help him through the long nights."

She was right, of course. Kneeling by the bed, I pushed my

hand in between the mattress and the box spring. I felt around, which wasn't too easy as Sophie was still lying on the bed. I found the well-thumbed magazine, pulled it out, and handed it to her. Smoothing it out, she said, "How long have you had this?"

"Five years. I walked past the shop a hundred times before I had the courage to go in. I bought a new comb and a family-size chocolate bar so it didn't look like I'd just gone in to get this."

She leafed through the magazine, looking at the girls on display. I felt a mix of emotions. I was embarrassed. This was a part of me I'd never wanted to share with anyone. There was also something exciting about seeing Sophie dressed this way casually perusing a porn mag. If she discovered she liked it, maybe it was something we could enjoy together. "Who's your favorite?" she asked.

I leaned across her to turn over a few pages. I was very familiar with this magazine and knew exactly what I was looking for. "Her," I said. There was a double page spread of a girl called Josephine, or, at least, that was the name she used when posing nude. She had long brown hair and blue eyes. She wasn't plump but there were healthy curves to her body. Her breasts were small and pert. The magazine was old enough that she still had a well-trimmed patch of brown pubes between her legs. Her pussy lips were tantalizingly suggested at rather than on display.

Sophie looked at the photos. "What do you like so much about her?"

I had to be honest. "It's her face."

"I'm not sure she'd thank you for saying that. She's showing you all her private parts and you're focused on the thing everyone gets to see."

"Don't get me wrong. I love her body and there are lots of things I would like to do with it . . . ." I paused. Maybe this wasn't something I should have been admitting to my girlfriend. I should have been saying, "I didn't even notice Josephine had a body because I only have eyes for you." It was a bit late to try that, so I said, "Her face looks patient, like she'd be understanding with someone who wasn't too experienced."

"I agree, she looks lovely," said Sophie. "So it's a pity you've got a bitch like me in your bed." She put the two pages together and pulled them out of the magazine with a jerk of her hand. In the excitement of looking at porn with my girlfriend, I'd forgotten the original purpose of this.

Holding the pages in both hands, she looked at me. "Please don't," I said, instinctively. I'm not sure how much I meant it and how much I was playing my part in the game.

With a sexy punk sneer, she ripped the pages into small pieces. I felt sorry to say goodbye to Josephine. Before I got with Sophie, I'd had a longstanding dream of Josephine sitting next to me on an airplane. She'd like my face as much as I liked hers and we'd be together ever after. Part of me hated Sophie for willfully destroy-ing something I loved. A much larger part of me found Sophie even more alluring now. She did things other people wouldn't even dream of. It made her more dangerous and exciting.

It was the part of me that hated her which pushed her onto her back. I lifted her skirt up to her waist. I thought about doing still more damage to her stockings by tearing a hole in the crotch. I settled for pulling them down roughly. I wondered briefly if punk Sophie had her pubes in a Mohican or maybe dyed green, but they were the same as normal. Without any foreplay, I pushed my cock into her cunt and started fucking her angrily. The fire in her eyes told me she was enjoying this new side to me. "There's something else punks love to do," said Sophie. "Come here."

I moved my face closer to hers as she puckered her lips. I assumed she was going in for a kiss. I didn't realize kissing was such an important part of punk life. I made the mistake of closing my eyes. There was a sound like a sudden escape of air and some-thing hit my left cheek. I opened my eyes just as Sophie puckered her lips again. This time, I saw the spit coming. It landed squarely on my nose, which I guess meant she'd scored a bullseye.

I was learning important lessons about sex and the way it could transform bad into good. Someone spitting in your face is disgusting, but if you're sufficiently turned on, it becomes erotic. Jealousy is a negative emotion but can be indistinguishable from lust.

I did nothing to avoid the hail of saliva shooting out of my girlfriend's mouth. In fact, I opened my eyes and mouth to give her more things to aim at. When I felt her spit in my mouth, I swallowed it. The realization I was doing something so dirty pushed me over the edge and I came. My orgasm calmed me down a little. I wanted to prove to Sophie that all the things she'd done during the evening hadn't dented my love for her even a little bit. I slid down her body and licked my punk girl's pussy until she screamed, "FUCK!"

The evening had been both physically and emotionally taxing. I lay next to her and we fell asleep for a while. She was looking at me when I woke up. "Any regrets?" she asked me.

I was happy to lose Josephine if I could be with such an exciting real-life woman so I shook my head.

"Peter, are we *both* perverts?" she asked.

"I certainly hope so," I replied.

TWELVE

PETER

I LOVED BEING WITH SOPHIE EVEN WHEN we weren't doing anything. Often we lay on the bed, studying or reading. Even working on a dull assignment was turned into a sensuous experience by the scent of her. Much as I liked these moments of simple togetherness, I was young and horny. Sex was never far from my mind. Even if we weren't doing it, I was keen to talk about it. "Er . . . Sophie," I began, tentatively.

She looked up from her book and said, "Hmm?"

I was realizing timing was everything when it came to discussing certain matters. She didn't want our relationship to be all about sex and sometimes wanted to talk about other things. She'd tell me to take a cold shower if she wasn't in that place. Looking into her eyes, I saw a glint of mischief, so I decided to chance it. "Sophie, you know when you danced with that guy the other night?"

"Oh, here we go," she said, but she smiled rather than rolling her eyes, so it seemed okay to continue.

"Would you like to play a little game some time?"

"I like games," she said, noncommittally.

"Maybe we could go out one evening . . . to a bar, or a club,

or somewhere. You could wear something revealing, low-cut perhaps, or even see-through. You'd score a point for every guy who
checks you out."

"What do points make?" she asked, with a grin.

"Anything you want them to. How about each point earns you
five minutes of me being your sex slave?"

She leaned forward and gave me a condescending kiss on the
top of my head. "You're pretty much my full-time slave anyway,
Peter. How about this? For every point I score, I can either spank
you five times or make you do something humiliating."

My heart beat faster. "Like what?" I wanted to know.

She gave an evil chuckle. "There's only one way to find out, isn't
there? So, Peter, are you going to pay to play?"

I was nervous but turned on. It was a mixture of feelings I was
getting used to. There was only ever going to be one answer. "I'm
in!"

SOPHIE

PETER AND I WENT SHOPPING AGAIN. It felt like a naughty little
adventure, buying clothes for me to attract other men with. We
went to a number of shops. I wanted to be noticed, but not arrested
for indecent exposure, so there was a delicate balance to be struck.
Nature has not equipped me to be an exhibitionist. My little boobs
do not automatically demand attention. Eventually, we chose a
black bra that pushed them together and up. I'd never had a cleavage before and I liked how it looked. We also decided on a sheer
navy blue blouse. It wasn't quite transparent but the black orbs of
my breasts in their bra were visible through the material. After we'd
chosen my outfit, I didn't even make a feint toward my purse. I
simply handed the clothes to Peter, knowing he had to be the one
to pay for them. From early on, I had a cuckoldress's instincts.

Not surprisingly, Peter wanted to have sex when we got back to my room. I kissed him a couple of times to get him even more worked up, then pushed him away. I wanted him in a high state of arousal and frustration. He watched as I got ready, putting on the clothes he'd bought and applying my make up. At one point I chided him, "Don't get too excited, Peter. You know this isn't for you." That seemed to turn him on even more.

My excitement gave way to unease as we left the building. I'd heard stories about men who had assaulted women because they were 'asking for it' by the way they dressed. Peter wouldn't be much good at defending me if I got into trouble, which was why I'd decided to go to a student bar called The One-Eyed Jack at the other side of town. It would be full of horny young people but I hoped—naïvely perhaps—that an educated crowd would be safer than a group of bikers or truck drivers. As we walked into the bar, I was shocked at seeing it full of real people. You might think of course they were real, but it still jarred me. Up until then, it had been a fantasy. I had been dressing up to attract the attention of nameless, faceless people who had no existence outside our imaginations. Suddenly, I was surrounded by people who all had faces and, presumably, names. As I'd predicted, most were about our age. There were a couple of older guys—middle-aged men who'd combed over their bald patches and sucked in their paunches, trying to convince themselves they could still attract women in their twenties. When they looked at me, I felt uncomfortable. Other guys made eye contact with me before their gaze scanned my body, taking moments to check out the size of my boobs, the curve of my hips, the length of my legs. My feminist sensibilities told me I was being a bad sister. I was presenting myself as a sex object to a group of men and for what? To satisfy another man's desire. On the other hand, it was kind of nice to have so many appreciative glances coming my way. I'd always been the nerdy girl who was overlooked by the boys. This was my time. The ugly duckling had been transformed into the swan of the bar by dint of a push-up bra and a sheer blouse. One guy clearly liked what he saw. He was a cute guy with glasses but the body under his white shirt showed he spent almost as much time working out as reading. The old me would have slunk past such a guy, assuming he was out of my league. With my newly boosted confidence, I held his gaze and looked at him right back. He didn't come over. He nodded and moved on.

Peter and I didn't sit down as I wasn't about to hide any part of my body under a table top. He bought us a glass of wine each and we leaned our backs against the bar, looking out at the room. Sometimes I held his hand, sometimes not. I wanted to see if more men checked me out when I wasn't obviously there with someone. My findings were inconclusive, but it didn't seem to make much difference. Men were happy to look at me whether I was touching my boyfriend or not. I liked that some of the guys were clearly sporty types. Maybe I wouldn't have to stick to geeks in the future. After twenty minutes, I finished my drink and put it on the bar behind me. The music was loud and Peter had to lean toward me and shout in my ear, "Do you want another one?"

I shouted back at him, "What do you want to happen this evening?" He paused and frowned. He'd had this image in his head of me in slutty clothes with guys looking at me lustfully. He hadn't thought through what, if anything, was going to happen next. I leaned in again and shouted, "Do you want me to flirt with any of these guys? See if one of them will buy me a drink?"

"Is that what you want?"

I never like it when a question is answered with another question. "It's a step backwards. Last time, I danced with a guy. This time it's look but don't touch."

"Are you enjoying it?"

"I like them looking."

"I like looking at them looking," he replied.

"Do you want to take things further?"

"Do you?"

This was becoming annoying. Partly to show my irritation at Peter's constant passing the buck, I flashed what I hoped was a seductive smile all over the room. It didn't take me long to catch the eye of a tall, dark-haired man with a blue fisherman's sweater stretched over well-developed shoulders. He looked back at me for long enough to show he was interested. I beckoned him over with a slight tilt of my head. "Hi," he shouted into my ear. "My name's Andy. Can I buy you a drink?"

"I'd prefer a dance," I shouted back.

"You sure you don't mind, buddy?" he asked Peter.

"Don't worry about Peter," I said. "He's my gay best friend. He's far more interested in you than me."

Peter blushed scarlet. Andy gave him a commiserating smile. "Sorry, can't help you there." Turning back to me, he said, "You, on the other hand . . .." He led me onto the dancefloor. He didn't waste any time jiggling in front of me. Putting his arm round my waist, he drew me to him. He wasn't much taller than me and our faces were only an inch apart. As he tilted his head to the right, it felt natural for me to do the same. Suddenly, our lips were together. They were different from Peter's. It took me a while to process whether that was good or not. My brain took a moment to remind me I was kissing another man while my boyfriend watched from the bar. Little Sophie was taking it to the next level. We kissed for a few minutes. I turned him around so I could give Peter a wanton look over Andy's shoulder. Peter was watching us with wide eyes and open mouth. "Do you want to sit down for a while?" Andy asked me.

Suddenly, I felt guilty—not about the effect on Peter, but on Andy. It was wrong to let him hope something might happen between us when I was using him to turn on my boyfriend. What could be my excuse? A sudden headache? Is that the time, I'm expecting an important phone call? In the end, I gave Andy a final peck on the lips and said, "I've got to go. Thanks for the dance." I walked away quickly before he had time to ask for my number. I went back to Peter. "We're out of here," I told him. He had the sense not to argue with me and we were through the main door ten seconds later.

It was only when we got back to Peter's room that I realized going to the bar was little more than a warm-up for the main event of the evening. He kissed me and said, "You looked fantastic tonight."

"A lot of guys agreed with you there."

"How many points did you rack up?"

"Quite a few. Not forgetting the bonus points I got for actually kissing a guy."

"That was so hot," said Peter. "Did you enjoy it?"

"Oh yes," I said. "Andy's a handsome guy. Good kisser too."

Peter made a low growl of desire. "You're in the mood to torment me."

"Baby, I'm only getting started. Now, what do I get for so many points? What are you going to do for me?"

"It's more what are you going to do *to* me."

A wave of sex washed over me. Peter wanted me to dominate him again. I was starting to like the idea of myself as the cruel and ruthless mistress. I was on the point of asking him what he had in mind, then I remembered I was the dominant one so it was my choice. I sat on the bed and looked at Peter, sternly. "Take off all your clothes." He undressed quickly and left his clothes in the corner of the room. It felt good to be fully clothed in the room with a naked man. After an evening of being watched, I enjoyed being the watcher. My eyes scanned Peter's body. It gave me an idea. "Are you ready for your first task?" He nodded and I said, "Tell me everything that's wrong with your body. How would you change it to make it worthy of me?"

The question had thrown him and he wasn't sure how to respond. "Well, my shoulders could be a bit bigger."

"A bit? I like manly men with broad shoulders and thick arms, not a slope-shouldered wimp with a couple of twigs hanging down." I couldn't resist adding, "More like Andy."

"I guess my chest could be bigger too."

"No one has ever asked you what your bench is. You'd have trouble pressing a carton of orange juice."

"You'd prefer it if I were a bit hairier too."

"Of course I would. I like real men with hairy chests. If I wanted smooth, soft skin, I'd be with a woman. Before you ask, no, I don't want to talk about me with another woman. I want to talk about your dick."

"You'd be happy if it were about two inches longer and twice as thick."

"It would be a start. All right, Peter. That's one point cashed in."

"Only one?"

"You're in for a long night. Lie on your front."

I always enjoyed spanking Peter. It wasn't much visually. I am a heterosexual woman, but one thing I will say for our straight male and lesbian friends is they have better butts to look at. The male posterior is not the most attractive body part in creation. Peter had left his clothes in a pile on the floor. I pulled his belt out from the loops in his pants and folded it double. As I walked back to the bed, something moved inside me. I've always been a gentle soul, the type who moves snails off the path so they don't get squashed. Now I found myself wanting to hurt Peter. I didn't understand why I felt like that. He was my boyfriend. There was a chance I might even love him. I felt powerful as I stood beside the bed. Old-school executioners used to touch the axe lightly against the condemned person's neck to get a feel for the distance. Peter winced as I touched the belt against his buttocks then breathed a sigh of relief as he realized there was no pain. Before the sigh was finished, I raised the belt quickly and brought it down on Peter's right buttock, making him scream. I was shocked by how much I liked hearing my boyfriend scream. I wanted to hear it again so tried to hit exactly the same spot, knowing it would be more tender. Now the initial shock had worn off, he didn't scream again, but moaned quietly into the pillow. I whipped him four more times before throwing the belt aside. His butt was striped with livid, red marks. Two bruises were coming through. There were real world consequences to his fantasy of my being a dominatrix. I remembered this butt was attached to a person I cared about. "Are you okay, Peter?" I asked, gently.

"Mm," he said into the pillow.

I wasn't sure what he meant so I said, "Turn over." He rolled onto his back and I gasped as I saw his cock, standing up hard and straight. "We can safely say you're okay," I said. He looked proud of it and gestured toward it. Maybe he was hoping I'd forget about everything else and just sit on his dick. To be fair, I was tempted, but now I knew he was as excited as me, I wasn't going to stop yet. Making my voice harsher again, I told him, "Go to the opposite corner. Lie on your front and crawl on your belly to me." He did it without question. I enjoyed his submission, but I saw him wincing. "What's wrong?" I asked.

"I'm getting a carpet burn on my cock," he said.

"That's the whole idea," I replied. It wasn't really, but it was a happy by-product.

"It hurts," he complained.

"It doesn't matter. It's only you."

"You . . ." he began.

I eyed him narrowly. "Me what, Peter?"

"Nothing," he said and carried on crawling.

"Didn't think so," I said. "Come and sit by me." When he was next to me on the bed, I squeezed his left bicep between my finger and thumb. With a contemptuous curl of my lip, I said, "Any of those guys in the bar could have fucked me and there's nothing you could have done to stop them. Any one of them could beat you."

"Do you want to see that happen?" Peter asked, almost in a whisper.

I put my finger on Peter's lips to stop him saying any more about the subject. "I reckon I've cashed in all my points now," I said. "Why don't you undress me and make love to me?" He looked pleased with that idea, but perhaps there was also a hint of disappointment in his eyes that the game was over . . . for now.

THIRTEEN

PETER

WHEN I STARTED SEEING SOPHIE, I kept her away from Mark. If I ran into Mark in the morning, I'd casually ask him what his plans for the day were. When he was planning a quiet evening in the pad, I arranged to go round to Sophie's place. If he was out and about, I could invite her round. In some ways, I wanted Mark and Sophie to get to know each other. They were the two most important people in my college life. It would be nice if we could all hang out together, but I knew what Mark was like. If even ten per cent of his bragging was true, he'd have no qualms about taking another guy's girlfriend, even if he was his friend. Being with Sophie had done wonders for my confidence, but I still knew most girls would pick Mark over me if offered a free choice. I also knew part of me would be disappointed if Mark *didn't* hit on Sophie. It would be like him saying she wasn't good enough for him.

One evening, I decided to see what would happen and I asked Mark if he could stick around when Sophie came over. He agreed like he didn't care much either way. We were in the den watching TV over a beer when Sophie arrived. Mark stood up in a gentlemanly fashion and shook Sophie's hand. "Nice to meet you properly at last," he said. "I've heard a lot about you."

"I've heard a few things about you too," she replied.

"Do you want some tea?" I asked Sophie, heading for the door.

"No, I'll have a beer," she said. I'd never seen her drinking beer before.

"A girl after my own heart," said Mark, opening the fridge beside his chair and taking out a can. He tossed it gently to Sophie and gave her an approving look when she caught it.

Mark sat back in the armchair. Sophie and I shared the couch. Mark was flicking between different sports. Sophie tried to engage him in conversation, but her questions were embarrassingly entry-level. "What's that guy's job? Why didn't he kick the ball when he had it?"

At first, he found the naïvety of her questions amusing. He soon let his irritation show and she kept quiet. The rest of the evening passed in awkward silence, apart from him asking us if we wanted more beer. I felt flat as I walked Sophie back to her building. I'd wondered what would happen when they met. Nothing much of anything had happened. I decided it didn't matter. I could divide my spare time between them—eighty per cent Sophie, twenty per cent Mark. That sounded fair.

When we arrived at her building, Sophie said, "You can come up if you want." Obviously, I did want. Shutting the door of her room behind her, she threw herself at me and pushed her tongue into my mouth. The intensity of the kiss was almost frightening. She pulled me onto her bed and took my clothes off so roughly there was a danger she'd tear something or at least rip off a few buttons. It was a price I was prepared to pay. If I reached for her clothes, she batted my hand away. I was naked while she was still fully-clothed. The vulnerability was exciting. Putting her hand on my erect cock, she rubbed the head between finger and thumb and said, "We're such a kinky couple, aren't we, Peter? We're fucking perverts."

She wasn't saying this like it was a bad thing so I nodded. "Yes, we are."

"You got turned on by watching me dancing with another guy. Then you got even more turned on by seeing another man kiss me . . ."

She trailed off and we lay there in silence, her fingers still around the head of my dick. We both knew what we had to talk about next, but neither of us was brave enough to say it out loud. Finally, I took a deep breath and asked, "Is there any part of you wants to go further?"

She bit her lip. "It seems inevitable. We can't talk about it forever without doing anything." I didn't see any compelling reason why we couldn't do just that. She continued, "Now might be the right time."

This struck me as a strange thing to say. Then I realized why she might be saying that. It made my heart skip with fear and my cock throb with desire at the same time. "Anyone you have in mind?" I asked. Then I added quickly, "Or are you imagining some random, generic guy?"

She looked at me curiously, like she wasn't sure if I was joking. "Don't you know? Mark, of course."

I hadn't known. I'd had no idea. "Really? You didn't have much to say to each other."

She kissed me on the nose. "What I have in mind doesn't involve much talking. I have you to talk to, Peter. You're not just my boyfriend. You're my best friend. Never doubt how much I appreciate that. Now make love to me while we both imagine Mark fucking me."

My cock was bigger than I'd ever seen it before so I had no trouble making love to her. I also knew it wasn't going to last long. I came inside her almost immediately. Without asking, I put my head between her legs and licked her urgently. I wanted us both in the clear-headed state that comes to those who have just had an orgasm. She came a lot more quickly than normal. I moved back up her body and lay with my head beside hers on the pillow. She had a knowing smile on her face. "Anything you want to talk about?" she asked.

"Was that one more fantasy or are you really thinking about Mark in that way?"

"Why not? He's a good-looking guy."

"He's my roommate. Can't you cast your net a little wider than the guy who lives in the same space as me?"

A wicked glint came into her eye. "Ever since you met him, you've envied him. He's your rival, but in an unfair battle. You can never compete with him. So how delicious would it be if he fucked your girlfriend?" Despite my attempt at post-orgasmic clarity, my cock started to come back to life as I heard her words. She noticed this and smiled. "The question is," she said, "how do we broach the subject with him?"

"I can't go up to him and say, 'Hey, dude, how's your day going? If you're not too busy one evening this week, any chance you could fuck my girlfriend?' "

"Maybe not, although I would love to see your face as you tell him that. We might have to do things the traditional way."

"Which is . . .?"

"We'll all have to get very, very drunk."

FOURTEEN

SOPHIE

PETER SAID BEER HAD NO EFFECT on Mark as he drank it every evening. We would need something stronger. Going out to pick up whiskey felt as naughty as buying the clothes I'd worn on our evening at The One-Eyed Jack. We were essentially buying a bottle of aphrodisiac. Peter had found out Mark was planning to stay in that night. We had our approach worked out. We were going to tell Mark we'd been out for a walk and had stumbled upon a fair. On a whim, we'd gone in and entered the raffle. Picture our surprise when we'd won a bottle of whiskey. We'd decided to share our good fortune with him. Would he join us in a glass if I promised not to ask stupid questions about sports this time?

Peter had his key in the door to the pad, as they called it, when he looked at me and said, "We don't have to do this, you know."

I kissed him on the lips and said, "Let's see how it goes. If things get awkward between him and us, we can duck into your room and it'll just be you and me. Next time we see him, we can blame it on the drink."

He still looked nervous as he opened the door. As it happened, we didn't need our story. Mark looked up as we came in, saw the bottle in Peter's hand, and said, "Hey! Peter and Sophie are here and they are ready to party!"

We also had three plastic cups with us. It was a good thing we hadn't used our story. It might have been difficult to convince him we'd also won some plastic cups at the fair. Peter poured a glass for each of us and we sat in the den. Mark was in the armchair with the best view of the TV. Peter and I sat on the couch. I was deliberately wearing clothes that suggested sex was the last thing on my mind. I was dressed for a countryside walk in a dark green blouse and blue jeans. I undid the top button of my blouse, but it didn't break much ice. We had started the drink flowing, but we still had to come up with the words. "So, Mark," I began, "have you got a girlfriend?"

I immediately regretted this as he gave me a look suggesting I knew as much about him as I did about sports. Even Peter rolled his eyes slightly. "The day I get a girlfriend is also the day I get a walking frame," said Mark. "It'll mean I've admitted I'm too old for this kind of life. I hope that won't be for at least another thirty years."

"No shortage of female company though," said Peter, with a hint of hero worship in his voice.

"The college years chapter of my autobiography will not be dull," Mark confirmed.

"What's your type?" I asked, with a forlorn hope that his preference would be for nerdy girls with glasses and a characterful nose.

He gave me a look only a little less patronizing than the one before. "A guy says he has a type to justify settling for someone. That never happens with me. When I get tired of a blonde, I move to a brunette. If the Scandinavian goddess isn't working for me anymore, I transfer my affections to the Asian babe."

Peter and I fully intended to take advantage of Mark's lifestyle, but there was something I needed to ask. "Isn't it wrong, moving from one girl to another?"

I got the feeling he'd answered such questions before because his answer sounded well-rehearsed. "I don't lead anyone on with false promises. I make it clear to every woman her time with me is limited. I'm not *the one*. I'm a pleasant diversion on life's journey. I will be an erotic memory a woman can use to take her mind off her husband."

"What if you meet a girl who makes you want to forget about all the rest?"

"Can you imagine a flavor of ice cream so good you never want to try any other flavor again?" My feminist part told me I should be repelled by this display of toxic masculinity. Once again, though, my horny side got the better of me and I couldn't help but be turned on by Mark's bad boy talk. I let out an involuntary little moan of desire. I thought it was quiet enough to go unnoticed, but Mark smiled. "Why? Could *you* make me forget all the rest?"

I hadn't expected him to be so bold. It's strange the way instincts kick in at times like this. My hands automatically rose up into a dismissive gesture and I prepared to say, "Oh no! Nothing like that! I'm only asking." Then I remembered I *was* interested, and said, "Maybe I could try." Even as I was saying it, it sounded like the lamest attempt at seduction ever.

Fortunately, Mark took over at that point.

MARK

SOPHIE WAS CUTE ENOUGH IN HER dorky way. I could imagine her playing the scientist in a TV show. She'd take her glasses off and shake out her hair. She still wouldn't be a supermodel, but she'd give geeky guys something to think about during the long nights. What I liked most about her, obviously, was that she was Peter's girlfriend. It would add an interesting dynamic to my roommate relationship with him. We'd be sitting around, watching TV, talking about our day. Always in the back of his mind would be the knowledge I'd fucked his darling girlfriend.

When Peter and Sophie sat with me in the den and stammered out their request, I wasn't surprised. I resisted the temptation to say, "What took you so long?" I moved sideways in my chair and patted the empty space. Sophie looked nervous but excited as she sat next to me. I breathed in. I always enjoy the smell of a new woman's perfume. "I'm going to kiss you now, Sophie. It's going to be a long, passionate kiss." We rotated toward each other in the chair. I put my hand behind her head and pulled her face to mine. Our mouths touched and I immediately put my tongue between her lips. They parted with no resistance. My tongue circled hers. I tasted the whiskey on her mouth. Underlying that was a pleasing sweetness. She let me kiss her rather than kissing me back. I kissed her until a shiver ran through her body. I moved my lips away from her and looked at Peter, to see his reaction to part of my body entering his girlfriend. He was staring with wide eyes and an even wider mouth. "Stand up," I said to Sophie. She frowned. She hadn't expected that to be the next move, but did as she was told. "You too, Peter." He stood up. "Peter, pop open the button of Sophie's jeans and put your hand down her panties so you can feel her pussy. Don't stimulate her in any way. That's not what this is about. Place the flat of your hand over her lips and curl your middle finger into her hole." He was shaking so much it took him a while to undo her button. They were both breathing heavily as his hand disappeared down the front of her jeans. When he looked at me for further instructions, I judged his hand was in place. "How's your girlfriend's pussy, Peter?" I asked him.

His voice was little more than a croak. "Wet."

"Is it wetter than you've ever known it before?"

He couldn't say anything so nodded.

"Sophie, what does it mean when your pussy is wet?" I asked.

"It means I'm sexually excited," she said.

"Is it your boyfriend touching you that's exciting you?"

She looked at Peter, bit her lip, then said, "No."

"What's making you excited?"

"You," she said.

"Sophie, do you want me to fuck you?"

"Yes, yes, I do."

PETER

Hearing Sophie ask Mark to fuck her was like the jump scare in a horror movie. I knew it was coming, but that didn't stop it from being a shock. Without doing her button up again, she walked to where Mark was sitting and looked at him, waiting to see what would happen next. He looked past her and spoke to me. "It's better if you go for a walk."

"I'll be okay," I protested.

"Maybe later," said Mark. "Not the first time."

"How long do you need?"

Mark shrugged. "Who can say? Give us an hour to be on the safe side." Sophie looked impressed.

"But–"

Sophie came back to me and gave me a hug. "Give us a bit of space, babe. This is a big moment for Mark and me. It's better if we don't have an audience."

I could have protested some more, but it wouldn't have done any good. Mark and Sophie went into his room. He grinned at me as he closed the door. I had a strong urge to stay and listen, but it wasn't what they wanted. I put on my coat and left. As I walked around aimlessly, I told myself I'd better get used to being alone. When Sophie and I fantasized about her with another guy, I was still the focus of her attention. All her talk was about turning *me* on. As we turned fantasy into reality, the other guy would have her attention, at least while it was going on. I suddenly asked myself why we'd taken this step. Sophie and I had a good thing going. Why would we change our relationship by inviting someone else into it? I looked round a bookshop but didn't care about any of the books, so it killed less than five minutes. I thought about going to a café, but I was jittery enough without adding caffeine to the mix. I considered drinking something stronger, but the idea of me sitting at a bar, alone, while my girlfriend was with another man suddenly seemed unbearably sad. I walked as far north as I could, before walking back. Then I walked as far south as I could. With the hour almost up, I turned toward our block. I asked myself what I was hoping to find when I got back to the pad. Maybe Sophie would be waiting for me saying, "I couldn't do it, babe. It felt wrong letting anyone except you touch me. I'm yours and yours alone. Now, please take me to your bed." If that happened, I'd be massively relieved, but maybe also a little disappointed.

I pushed open our door with the trepidation of someone stepping into a murder scene. There was no sign of any disturbance in the den. "Is that you, Peter?" called Mark from his room. As it couldn't have been anyone else, he didn't wait for a reply. "Bring me a beer, would you?"

"One for me too," said Sophie from his room.

"Since when have you drunk beer?" I called to her.

"It's the new me," she said, which was as good an answer as any. I took three beers from Mark's little fridge. I figured I deserved one too. I took a moment to steady myself before I went into Mark's bedroom. I wasn't sure what scene of debauchery was waiting on the other side. I pushed open the door and was confronted with the most erotic sight I've ever seen. It's not so much what was on show as what was hidden. Sophie and Mark were sitting up in bed together. His chest, with its thick covering of dark hairs, was on display. She had demurely drawn up the sheet to cover her breasts. I interpreted this as her saying I wasn't allowed to see them. Just then, they belonged to Mark. He had the satisfied look of a man who had gotten exactly what he wanted. There was a smell of sex in the air. Genitals had become hot and sweaty in this room and semen had been spilled.

"You've been holding out on me, buddy," Mark told me. "You said your girlfriend was smart and funny. You didn't say she was also a ball of fire in the sack. One or two things we need to work on, but generally good."

I thought Sophie might be offended but she looked pleased at this positive assessment of her performance.

Mark took a chug of his beer and burped loudly. "Mark!" said Sophie. The look of affectionate reproach she gave him was exactly the one a girlfriend gives a boyfriend when he's being uncouth. This worried me as much as anything else they might have done.

"I could go again," said Mark. Turning his head toward Sophie, he asked, "Are you up for it?"

Trying to play it cool, she said, "Why not?" I had the feeling what she wanted to say was, "Yes! Yes! Please yes!"

"Why don't you go to your room for a while?" Mark suggested to me. "I need to fuck your girlfriend again, but this time, it'll be quick and nasty." Sophie gave a little moan at this prospect. "I'll send her back to you in fifteen or twenty minutes."

FIFTEEN

PETER

I SAT ON MY BED, STILL FULLY clothed. I had my ear against the wall, trying to listen to what was going on in Mark's room. I heard indistinct mumblings. The sound of Mark's door opening came through more clearly. Sophie came in. She was naked, carrying her clothes in a bundle. If she felt guilty, she didn't show it. "How you doing, babe?" she asked.

I decided to be honest. "I don't know. What about you?"

"Oh, I'm fine." Putting her clothes on the floor, she sat on the bed and took my hand in hers. "I'm your girlfriend and I've just had sex with another man. I'm a bad girlfriend." She let go of my hand and squeezed the bulge in my trousers. She grinned as she felt how hard I was. "You don't seem to mind."

"So . . . how was it?" I asked.

"You want to hear all about it?" she asked. Of course I did. If I couldn't watch, I at least needed to hear the post-match report. She was quiet for a while, not sure how to tell me, then the dam broke and she gushed, "Oh, Peter, it was great. Don't get me wrong, making love with you is nice. You're so kind and affectionate. Mark is not either of those things. Sex with him is like being caught up in a tornado. I had to brace myself."

My heart was beating so hard, I had to concentrate on keeping calm. "Tell me everything," I said quietly. "Start from the moment Mark closed the door to his room."

She took a deep breath and began. "I was standing in the middle of his room. He turned round from closing the door and came toward me. I was expecting him to kiss me again so I tilted my face up to his. Instead, he grabbed my shirt and pulled it." She bent and took her shirt from the bundle on the floor. Holding it up in front of me, she said, "Nearly all the buttons popped off."

"He's also done a bit of damage," I said, pointing to a tear an inch below the collar.

"That's where he grabbed it. His finger must have gone through. You'll have to get good at sewing or this is going to be expensive." I took note of the implication that it was going to happen again. I didn't have time to process it as she carried on, "He didn't waste much time looking, but squeezed my tits through my bra. He wasn't gentle." She arched her back, pushing her tits toward me. "Did he leave any traces?"

I examined her chest. "There are red finger marks on your left tit."

She nodded. "His right hand is pretty strong. I felt both his strong hands on my shoulders as he pushed me onto my knees. I knew what he wanted of course, so I undid his belt and pulled down his fly. He was wearing boxers under his jeans so I put my hand in and pulled out his cock." She paused, pupils dilated, mouth open. "Oh babe, his cock was so much . . . different from yours."

I knew she'd stopped herself at the last minute from saying 'better.' She was still walking the tightrope between nice girlfriend and cruel cuckoldress. "Different in what way?" I asked.

"Your cock reminds me of a baby mouse shading its eyes with its paws. It's cute and vulnerable." I'm not sure any man wants to hear his penis is vulnerable. "Mark's is thick and rough, like an old length of mooring rope." This didn't sound too complimentary either, but Sophie obviously approved. "It's beautiful," she added, dreamily, as if talking to herself. "But you already know that," she added.

"How would I know that?" I demanded.

"You share a room. You must have seen each other naked."

"We have separate bedrooms and a lock on the bathroom door. No, we haven't."

"I've a feeling you will soon," she said.

Banking this thought for future use, I asked, "How big was it? Show me on my cock."

I lay back on the bed and feverishly undid my trousers. My cock had been fighting for release and sprang gratefully out of captivity. It was at full size. Sophie placed her finger two and a half inches above my tip. "Mark's is about this long." She put her finger and thumb around my cock with a half inch gap on either side. "It's also this thick."

"So Mark's cock is bigger than mine," I said.

Sophie kissed me. "Oh yes, babe. Much bigger."

"So . . . you pulled out his horse cock . . .."

"That's a good way of describing it. I licked my lips to moisten them and put them round the head of his horse cock. I had to open my mouth so wide, my jaw cracked the way it did the first time we kissed, babe." I was touched she remembered that detail about us. "I licked the head for a while then moved my mouth down his shaft, trying to fit as much of it as possible in my mouth. I couldn't get it all the way in, but I hope he appreciated my efforts. Standing me up, he said, 'I want you naked. Now.' He didn't want any teasing. I had to take my clothes off as quickly as possible. Soon, I was in front of him without a stitch on. He led me to his bed and told me to get on all fours, pushing my ass up toward the ceiling. He knelt up on the bed and I felt his hands on my butt cheeks. His thumbs reached between my thighs to open up my pussy lips. I said something about a condom, but he told me not to worry about it. Obviously, that made me worry more, but I didn't have much time to dwell on it. I gasped as he pushed his cock inside me, but that was nothing to what happened next. I thought men liked to start slow and build up the pace. Not Mark. He pounded his cock into me hard and fast right from the first thrust, knocking all the air out of me. I struggled to catch my breath. It was like nothing I'd ever felt before, babe. A bit like being on a rollercoaster. Scary but such a rush. I didn't have too much time to get my head around what was happening. Before I knew it, I was cumming."

"It normally takes you a long time to get there," I said.

"Not with him, babe. I came on his cock and screamed so loud I'm surprised campus security wasn't knocking at the door. I thought he'd take that as his cue to cum and it would be over, but my orgasm didn't even break his rhythm. He kept on with his cock going in and out of my cunt. I was getting sore, which only made my pussy hyper-sensitive. I couldn't believe I'd be able to cum again so quickly, but, what can I tell you, that guy knows what he's doing. My second orgasm wasn't so noisy, but it was intense. I felt it in waves all through my body. I was pretty much wrung out. It meant he could focus on himself. He pulled his cock out of me and turned me onto my back. He had a condom already unwrapped and stashed under the bed. He bent to pick it up and put it over his cock in one expert movement. He was soon back inside me, but now he was taking his time, enjoying the feeling, even with a layer of latex in the way. We didn't kiss much, but he stroked my thighs. I put my arms behind my head."

I'd been hoping she'd kept at least one intimate detail of her body just for me, but apparently not. "He saw your armpits," I said.

"Yes, I caught him looking at them."

"Did he love them as much as me?"

"Not sure," she said, and quickly moved on. "He liked my tits, though. He kissed them all over and nibbled my nipples. You might be able to see his teeth marks on them." I had a look, but Sophie's nipples have natural puckering. It was hard to tell what might be a tooth mark. She continued, "Feeling him move inside me slowly was different, not as breathtaking but still so good. I would have cum again, but he reckoned I'd had enough for the moment. I felt him cumming so much I was afraid the condom would burst. He grunted with satisfaction and I'm glad I could make him feel so good. It didn't feel right for me to lie in his arms: that's what I do with you." It was good to know one thing at least was reserved for me. "We sat up in bed, not saying much, until you came back. As you saw, he soon got excited again."

"What happened after I came back in here?" I asked.

"He had another condom under his bed, so he doesn't lack for confidence. He put it on, then lay on his back with his cock standing up like a . . .."

She was struggling to find a simile so I suggested, ". . . like a huge erect cock?"

She nodded. "Exactly like a huge erect cock. I squatted over him and sat on his dick. My pussy lips were so sore."

"Let me see," I said. Sophie spread her legs and opened up her cunt with her two forefingers. Her lips were red and swollen. "Ouch, they look painful."

"It was worth it," she said, in a matter-of-fact way. "I'll need you to lick me over the next few days, as I'm still horny as hell, but don't count on fucking me any time soon." I settled for kissing her pussy while she finished her story. "I held the base of his cock and lowered myself onto it."

"Where did you learn to do that?" I had to ask.

She shook her head. "Not sure. Maybe it's instinct, a trick every woman is born knowing. I winced as his big cockhead touched my sensitive lips. Once he was inside, though, pleasure took over. I went up and down on his dick, finding the perfect rhythm for me. I rubbed my clit but mainly for him. I think guys like seeing a woman pleasuring herself. His cock inside me was enough to have me cumming again inside a couple of minutes. He took over and held onto my hips, lifting me up until his head was just inside me then slamming me down on him. If his cock had been in even slightly the wrong position, I'd have snapped it in two, but I trusted he knew what he was doing and went with it. I felt his cum pulsing into the condom, not as much as the time before, but still impressive. You know the rest because then I came in here. Well, Peter, you're all caught up. Any questions?" I had at least a thousand questions, but she didn't give me time to ask even one before saying, "Oh, I forgot to say: after I climbed off his dick, he told me I should go to my boyfriend because you might need some reassurance." It was nice Mark was considering my feelings. "I kissed him and thanked him."

After all I'd heard already, I didn't think anything could surprise me, but this hit me like an electric shock. "You thanked a man for fucking you."

"Yes, I did." She wrapped her hand around my cock and massaged it gently. "Your dirty, unfaithful girlfriend thanked your roommate for giving her the best fuck of her life." This was too much for me. My body jerked uncontrollably and my cum squirted into her hand. She sat up and looked at the ivory-colored mess in her hand. She started going for a Kleenex then changed her mind and wiped my cum over her tits. "I'm still yours, Peter," she said.

My cumming seemed to break the spell. She went back to being more like my Sophie. She took me in her arms and said, "I love you, Peter." It was the first time she'd said it. Of all the moments to choose! "Never doubt I love you, whatever I've done . . . or whatever I'm going to do," she added chillingly.

What else could I say except, "I love you too, Sophie." After all, it was the truth.

She smiled. "In spite of me being a cheating slut, or because of it?"

"There are so many reasons, but that is one of them," I admitted. Our lips met. Believe it or not, it was a genuinely romantic moment.

I felt my cock coming back to life as we kissed. We might have made love the way couples do but Mark's voice came through the bedroom door from the den. "If you lovebirds have finished whatever it is you're doing, could you come out here for a while?"

Sophie and I put our clothes back on. I'm not sure why she felt the need to cover up before seeing Mark. He was sitting in the chair, wearing just his boxer shorts. He directed us to the couch. "What we did was nice," he told Sophie. "We're going to do that again." I was annoyed by the way he simply assumed my girlfriend would want to have sex with him again. For all he knew, it was a one-time event, something she needed to get out of her system before going back to a conventional relationship with her boyfriend. At the same time, I kind of admired his confidence. Sophie looked relieved. Mark carried on, "I want to make sure there are no misunderstandings here. All I'm offering you is sex. There is no possible scenario in which we end up together."

Even Sophie was shocked by this display of Mark's rampaging ego, but all she said was, "I'm with Peter."

"I know," he said, "but when a woman's having great sex with a guy, sometimes she needs to justify it to herself by saying she's in love with him."

"That's not going to happen here," said Sophie.

"Just so we're clear. Now, on another point, there are a few changes you need to make. Someone like Peter is so happy to be in bed with a woman that he doesn't pay much attention to the wrapping. I am more discerning. Simple bra and panties that you get in a pack of five from the superstore won't cut it with me. I want to see you in high-quality lingerie, preferably French. Black and red are my favorite colors but I've no objection to virginal white."

"Okay," said Sophie, meekly. I had no complaints about this, either. I saw some erotic shopping trips in the next couple of days as Sophie and I picked out underwear to turn Mark on.

"The only thing I want to smell when I'm in bed with you is your perfume," Mark said. "You must shower before coming to see me, paying special attention to your feet, armpits, and pussy."

Sophie did bristle at this. "Peter likes my natural scents."

"Peter's a pervert," he replied. I couldn't argue, so said nothing. "Most important," said Mark, "is I don't have a *Planet of the Apes* fetish. Hairy women are a definite no-no." This showed a huge double standard coming from someone as hirsute as he was. "Make sure your armpits and pussy are smooth for me by next time."

This was Sophie's opportunity to look Mark defiantly in the eye and say, "My body, my choice, mister." What she actually said surprised both of us. "Could I have another look?" With a triumphant smirk, Mark stood up and dropped his shorts to his thighs. It was my first view of his cock. Even in repose and clearly worn out from strenuous activity, it was impressively long and thick. Sophie looked at it for a long time before saying quietly, "Anything you say, Mark."

SIXTEEN

PETER

THERE WAS A BATHROOM WITH AN actual bath in it along the hall from the pad. It was ten in the morning as I ran the bath, adding rose and geranium bath soak and a little de-stress bath oil for good measure. I made sure it was the perfect temperature. Sophie was standing behind me, holding a bag and wearing a broad towel which covered her body from the breasts to the midpoint of her thighs. As soon as her bath was ready, she took the towel off and looked at herself in the mirror above the basin. She put her hands behind her head and checked out her armpits.

"Come here, babe," said Sophie, turning to me with her hands still behind her head. "When I got out of bed this morning, I washed all the deodorant out of my armpits, then I went for a run. That was three hours ago, so my pits should be absolutely rank, the way you like them." My cock was already stirring from being in the same room as naked Sophie. At these words, it grew as much as it could within the confines of my jeans. "Do you want to kiss them?" she asked, which was a silly question. I put my arm round the small of her back and leaned in to her right armpit. I inhaled deeply, filling my nose with the hot musk of her sweat. I kissed every part of her armpit before using the flat of my tongue to lick it from bottom to top. She squeezed my bulge through my jeans. "Enjoy it while you can, babe," she said. "They'll never be like this again." I moved to her left armpit, kissing and licking it still more fervently. "All right, Peter, enough. You can have too long a goodbye." I straightened up and tried to kiss her but she backed away. "Ew," she said, "I don't want to taste my sweat on your lips. You need to hit the mouthwash." This left me with a dilemma. I wanted the taste of her armpits to linger forever, but I didn't want to go too long without kissing her.

She climbed into the bath and lay down to let the hot water soften the hair under her arms. She sat up and her hands went back behind her head. As I rummaged in the bag for a can of foam, I felt a mixture of sadness and excitement. On the one hand, I remembered the times I'd enjoyed her hairy pits. One time, she'd even oiled up her left pit and let me fuck it. At the same time, my cock was hard at the prospect of what was about to happen. My girlfriend was going to alter her body to make it more the way another man liked it. She was going to destroy something I loved to please someone else. "Are we really going to do this?" I asked.

"We've got to." I wasn't sure about that. The option of telling Mark to fuck off was there for us, but it wasn't what Sophie wanted. I squirted the shaving foam into her right armpit and gave it a moment to sink in. I took a razor out of the bag and dragged it through the foam. A clump of long hairs clung to the blade. I rinsed the razor in the bath water and applied it to her armpit three more times. I cleaned away the foam to reveal uneven patches of fuzz with a few rogue long hairs which had escaped the blade. Sophie looked down. "Keep going, babe. Mark wants it perfectly smooth." I was close to telling Mark where he could stick his wants, but I moved in for the detail work. Using the corner of the blade, I carefully trimmed away all the hairs. Sophie ran her finger down her armpit and declared herself satisfied. "Now the other one." After both her armpits were silky smooth, she held out her hand for the razor. "No offence, Peter, but I'd better do my pussy myself. You're so excited, you're shaking a little. There's not too much damage you can do under my arms, but I don't want you accidentally slicing my clit off." She took the razor. I expected her to kneel up in the bath to apply the foam, but she reckoned the hot water and bath oil were enough to soften her pubes. She used broad strokes on the thickest part of her bush on the mons. Little islands of hair floated to the surface and bobbed around. When it came to removing the hairs on her pussy lips, she used the blade with a surgeon's precision. As soon as she was happy, she pulled out the plug with her toe. By the time all the water had drained, she was hairier than when we started with the shavings clinging to her body. I used the shower attachment to clean her and helped her out of the bath. She gave a little squeak of surprise as she saw herself in the mirror. It was like when you don't recognize yourself after a haircut. It didn't look like her pussy without the crown of hair. She checked her armpits and grunted with approval. Reaching into the bag, she pulled out a can of deodorant and a perfume bottle. Mark had made her paranoid about her natural aromas so she sprayed half a can of deodorant under each arm. She aimed the perfume at her tits, belly, upper and lower back. "How do I look, babe?" she asked.

I preferred her hairy but, seeing her smooth and knowing *why* she was smooth, I thought she'd never looked sexier. "Fantastic," was the best I could say.

"How do I smell?"

To be honest, it was overpowering in a small college bathroom but it would dissipate during the walk back to the pad. "You smell like a woman ready for love."

I tried to put my arms around her but she pushed me away. "Sorry, babe, not now. This isn't for you." She wrapped the towel around herself again and picked up the bag.

A guy I didn't know walked past us as we went back to the pad.

He didn't seem to notice the woman dressed in nothing but a towel. He sniffed the air and said, "It smells like a Turkish cat house in here." I'd never been to a Turkish cat house, so I couldn't comment.

Arriving back in the pad, we found Mark waiting for us. He knew what we'd been doing and we'd agreed he'd be back by eleven. Without any preamble, Mark said. "Show me." Sophie let the towel fall to the floor and stood in front of him, naked. Mark moved in like he was inspecting the troops. If there'd been anything wrong with her body, he would have told her to drop and give him twenty. Fortunately, he was satisfied. "You've done a good job," he said, also favoring me with an approving nod. "Let's go into Peter's room and have sex in his bed." My mouth fell open at this suggestion. If he was inside my girlfriend, it shouldn't matter if he was also inside my bed, but it was an added violation of me and my space. In spite of this—or because of it—Sophie liked the idea. She gave a little growl of desire and followed Mark into my bedroom. He looked at me over his shoulder and said, "Come on, Peter. You can watch this time."

MARK

IT'S ALWAYS STRANGE, GOING INTO SOMEONE else's bedroom. There are different smells in the air and nothing is ever where I would put it. I've always known it's an important part of the cuckold experience. The couple's safe space needs to be invaded so every time they make love or settle down to sleep, they know another man's been there. Sophie was already naked so I put my arms around her. She'd listened to what I'd said about perfume and the strong floral scents were intoxicating. I felt up her ass. Thin girls often have boring, flat butts that are just a continuation of their legs. Sophie's buttocks had a nice curve to them and were good to cup. A lot of this was to ease Peter in gently to seeing me touch his girlfriend. "Take your glasses off," I told her. "I want you completely naked." She took them off and put them on Peter's bedside table. I moved my hand up to the back of Sophie's head and pulled her face toward mine. Planting my lips against hers, I stuck my tongue into her mouth intrusively. I wanted her to be shocked by the sudden incursion. She made a high-pitched noise with surprise in it but also a lot of arousal. I kissed her for a few minutes. I liked the way Sophie tasted. She had a fresh, slightly sweet taste, like melon. Peter had already seen me kiss his girlfriend, but he stared at us, wide-eyed and open-mouthed.

"Undress me," I told Sophie. She unbuttoned my shirt. Pushing it aside, she bent to kiss my left nipple and ran her nose through the hair on my chest. "You like my hairy chest, don't you, Sophie?" I asked.

Without moving her face away, she nodded and said, "Mm mm."

"Makes a change from Peter, doesn't it?"

This time she looked up into my eyes and said, "You've got a man's body."

Peter gave out a little lustful groan. I looked over at him. He was standing just inside the door. The look on his face was one I'd seen in other cuckolds. For him, the only thing worse than watching me fuck his woman would be *not* watching me fuck her.

Sophie removed my shirt and took the opportunity to run her hands along my shoulders, gently squeezing my muscles. She got on her knees and undid my belt buckle. Pulling down my jeans and shorts, she gasped as my cock sprang out and hit her in the face. I turned slightly so Peter could get a good view of what would shortly be penetrating his girlfriend. Sophie knew what she had to do. Putting her lips round my cock, she teased the head with her hot breath. Then her tongue flicked the tip. She opened her mouth wide and took my length as deep as she could. The way she moved her lips and tongue around my cock wasn't exactly expert but I appreciated her enthusiasm. I gave Peter a thumbs up to let him know his girlfriend was performing satisfactorily. I didn't want it to go on for too long, though. She and Peter had gone to a lot of trouble to get her body the way I liked it. I wanted to enjoy it. I took my cock out of her mouth and stepped out of my jeans and shorts. I took my socks off because I'm a classy guy.

Now we were both naked, it was time to take her to Peter's bed. He'd left his pajamas under the pillow, which is an annoying habit so I put them on the floor by the bed. I laid Sophie on her back. I'm not generally much of a pussy licker, but I had to have a closer look at her newly hairless vulva. It was beautifully smooth. She shivered as I kissed her sensitive mound. She had a few spots of shaving rash, but I didn't hold it against her. I flicked my tongue over her clit, to make her moan. I lay on top of her, kissed her neck a couple of times, then began to maneuver my cock toward her pussy. This caused a, "Hey!" from Sophie.

Peter joined in with a, "Hang on a minute!"

"What?" I asked, innocently.

"Have you got a condom?" asked Peter.

"They're all in my room," I replied.

"I'll go and get them, shall I?" he asked.

"No, Peter, you won't."

Sophie said, "Peter has some in his bedside drawer. Do you want one of those?"

"No, I'm not going to use one this time. Your pussy looks so perfect now that I have to feel it round my cock with nothing in the way."

"Isn't it . . . dangerous?" stammered Sophie.

I got off her, sat back on my heels, and looked at her calmly. "We can stop if you want." I love this moment. It's where a woman asks herself how much she's prepared to risk for my cock.

Sophie's struggle lasted only a couple of seconds. "No, I don't want to stop."

This was what I needed to hear. It was good for Peter to hear it too as it drilled into him what a hold I had over his girlfriend.

I got on top of her again. She tried to guide me in, but I brushed her hand away. "I don't need any help." My cock is a heat-seeking missile. I pride myself on hitting the target first time every time. I penetrated her and took a moment to appreciate the sensation of Sophie's cunt around my naked cock. She felt good. She was hot and tight. I could tell from her face she was enjoying it—not only me inside her, but my strong arms around her, my control of the situation. She put her hands behind her head so I could see her freshly shaven armpits. She finally looked the way a woman should. I kissed her pits as I started a slow rhythm of moving my cock in and out of her, withdrawing to the tip before pushing my full length back in. Sophie bit her lip. Her body squirmed under me. After only a couple of minutes, she was getting close to cumming. Ordinarily, I would have made her wait. I like a woman to be desperate for an orgasm by the time I finally let her have one. This time, I wanted Peter to see how easily I made his girlfriend cum. I increased the speed of my thrusts. She threw back her head, eyes rolling, mouth open. Her strong young cunt muscles squeezed my cock as she came with a strangled shout. She laid her head flat on the pillow with the biggest grin I'd ever seen. Turning to Peter, I said, "She looks happy, doesn't she?" He didn't say anything but only nodded. He looked broken, which is something I like to see in a cuckold, even if he is my friend. I pulled out of Sophie's cunt. Both of them were relieved I hadn't cum in it. She put her hand on my cock as if jerking me off would be enough. I shook my head. "Has a man ever cum in your mouth?"

She was torn between not wanting to appear unworldly and not wanting to come across as a slut. "No, never," she said.

"Would you like it to happen?"

Peter chimed in. "She's not into that."

I gave him a stern look. "Let your girlfriend speak for herself, Peter."

"I wouldn't mind . . . trying it . . . some time . . ." she said, hesitantly.

"Sophie, do you want me to cum in your mouth?" I asked her.
"Yes . . . yes, I do."

I had only one word to say. "Beg."

She looked surprised but determined to meet this new challenge. "Please, Mark," she said. "I love your cock so much, I want it everywhere, especially in my mouth. I need to taste it. I'm sure your cum is like nectar. Shoot it into my mouth and watch me swallow it all like a greedy bitch. Please, Mark, cum in my mouth. Do it as a favor to me."

I lay on the bed with my cock pointing at the ceiling. Sophie knelt between my legs and put her lips around my cock again. It felt nice but her inexperience was soon apparent. I knew I couldn't cum from the attention of her lips and tongue. I grabbed a handful of her hair and held it in position. Using my well-developed leg and core muscles, I moved my cock up and down, fucking Sophie's soft mouth until I pumped three big loads of my seed into it. I assumed she didn't know the cum-in-mouth etiquette, so I talked her through it. "Keep your lips tight around my cock, Sophie. Don't break the seal. Move your mouth slowly up to the tip. Close your mouth the second you get free of the tip. Some will spill but keep it to a minimum. Then kneel up on the bed and wait for further instructions." As soon as she was kneeling up with her mouth clamped shut, I told her, "Tip your head back slightly. Show Peter your mouth full of another man's cum." She opened her mouth. Her tongue was covered in my thick, white semen. Most of it had pooled in the back of her mouth. Peter stepped forward so he could see better. He was shaking and breathing heavily. He'd had about all he could take for one day, but there was one task he still had to perform. "OK, Sophie," I said, "close your mouth and swallow my load. Then show us both your empty mouth." She looked nervous but closed her mouth, steeled herself as if about to take a dose of medicine, then gulped it down. She opened her mouth. Peter staggered a little. This was no magic trick. His girlfriend had just swallowed another man's cum. A bit of it had dripped down

Sophie's chin. "Peter," I said, "kiss your girlfriend. Reassure her. While you're doing it, clean up her chin, will you?"

I thought maybe he'd reach for a tissue, but he was starting to understand what's required of a cuckold. He leaned over the bed and licked her chin clean with two short strokes of his tongue. Then he kissed her tenderly and said, "I love you."

She gazed into his eyes and said, "I love you too, babe." It was touching. I was almost sad to break the spell. As she started getting off the bed, I pointed to my cock. "There's still some cum on it," I told her.

She knew immediately what was required of her. They were both learning fast. "Oh, sorry," she said. Pushing her hair back, she bobbed her face down to my crotch and licked up the blobs of semen. I let her get off the bed, but my cock was still shiny. I picked Peter's pajama top off the floor and used it to wipe my dick with. As I put it back under his pillow, I gave Peter a wink. Yes, I was being obnoxious but deliberately so. I'd go back to being Peter's friend soon.

PETER

ONE THING I HADN'T APPRECIATED ABOUT the reality of inviting another man into our bed was the intimate knowledge I'd get of him. Although Mark and I lived in close proximity, he'd always changed in his own room. Before he started having sex with my girlfriend, I didn't know he had so much hair on his chest or that the muscles in his buttocks were so well-defined. The thing which surprised me the most, despite Sophie's description of it, was his cock. I was ready for it to be bigger than mine, but I was surprised at how different it was: powerful, potent, and animalistic; while mine is unobtrusive and polite. Sophie's reaction to sex with him was also humbling for me. She grunted when I made her cum.

With Mark, she let out something more like a roar. If a woman could only have sex once more in her life, I knew it would be with someone like Mark in preference to someone like me. I tried to accept it as the natural order of the world. He was good-looking, athletic, and attractive, while I was . . .. Well, I was fairly sure I was smarter than him, but that wasn't much comfort.

Sophie realized I needed something from her. She came over to me and put her arms around my waist. I hugged her close. Her naked body felt good.

"I'll leave you two alone," said Mark. "I've got one more thing to say before I go. These sheets are not to be changed for the next week. As you go to sleep every night, I want you to be reminded your girlfriend is a cheating slut."

He went out. Sophie led me over to the bed which smelled strongly of infidelity. We lay down. She looked at me nervously, wondering what my reaction would be now the excitement had worn off. It hadn't worn off for me as I was the only one who hadn't cum yet. Nevertheless, I knew the first thing I had to do was reassure her. I put my arm around her and gathered her in so her head was on my chest. She snuggled in to me gratefully, tickling my nose with her hair. My motives in hugging her weren't entirely altruistic. As I held her, I breathed in deeply. I could smell him on her. He'd marked—or Marked—her with his scent. The dominant aroma was his strong cologne with its notes of leather and tobacco. There was also a mixture of sweats—his mixed with hers. I rolled onto my side so her head slid off my chest and onto the pillow. I lay facing her. So much had changed in such a short time that it was almost a surprise to see she was still my pretty, nerdy girlfriend. She reached over to the bedside table to get her glasses. Putting them on, she looked even more like Sophie and less like the porn star she'd just resembled. I put my lips onto hers. I managed only a fleeting peck before she drew her head back and covered her mouth. "Do you want me to brush my teeth before you kiss me again?"

"No, you're all right," I said.

"If you're not turned on anymore, it might be a bit weird for you to taste him on me."

I *was* still turned on but, instead of telling her that, I said, "There's nothing that isn't weird about this situation."

She laughed. There was a lot of relief in the laugh. "Ain't that the truth!" she said. "So it's okay to kiss you?"

"Sophie, it's always okay to kiss me."

As soon as she had the green light, she kissed me as aggressively as Mark had kissed her. She pushed her tongue into my mouth, now clearly wanting me to taste Mark on her. I wasn't sure I could taste his cock, but his cum was still strong in her mouth. I tasted its sour saltiness. I'd tasted my own jizz a few times, but always had the disadvantage of having just cum so I wasn't turned on. Now, I was more aroused than I'd ever been in my life so I liked the taste of his cum.

She reached down to find my cock, but I gently pushed her hand away. I knew any friction would make me cum in a second, and I wanted to spend hours forensically quizzing her on every detail of what had happened. I wasn't sure how to get started on this. Fortunately, Sophie said, "Well, I did it. I fucked another man in front of you."

"I wasn't sure it would ever happen in real life, but you did it."

"Do you hate me?"

I kissed her again. Almost as a reflex, she put her tongue in my mouth so I could taste Mark's cum. It was supposed to be a reassuring rather than erotic kiss, but I wasn't complaining. I made sure my words were unambiguous. "I didn't think it was possible to love you any more than I already did. Seeing you with Mark reminded me of how sexy you are."

SEVENTEEN

MARK

I WENT INTO THE PAD AND FOUND Sophie on the couch in the den, watching something on TV which featured bad special effects. She was nursing a cup of tea and wearing one of Peter's shirts. Her caramel-colored legs were bare. She looked up as I came in, blushed prettily, and said, "Hey."

"Hey, where's Peter?"

"He had to go to the library. You don't mind me being here, do you?"

"No, it's cool. What are you watching?"

"*Doctor Who*, the original series from the 1970s."

I shook my head. "You are such a geek."

"It's a classic," she protested.

I went into my room and started to get changed. I was going to break with tradition and do some work, but Sophie's legs kept coming back into my mind. It seemed a waste to have her in the next room and not do anything about it. Shirtless, I went back into the den and sat next to her. She looked at me as I sat down. "Keep watching," I said. I put my hand on her thigh and caressed it gently. She parted her legs slightly and my hand slid between them. As my hand crept up, I felt her slit already moistening. "No panties," I said.

"Nope," she replied.

I pulled my pants and shorts to my knees, releasing my erect cock. I patted my lap. Sophie slid across the couch. I helped her lift herself up and maneuvered her into place so my dick easily slid up into her cunt. I enjoyed again the warm tightness of her pussy around my shaft. "What's happening in the show?" I asked into Sophie's ear.

"You want to talk about it now?" she asked, surprised.

"Tell me everything." It was strange pillow talk, but I knew what I was doing.

"The Doctor and his companions have transmatted to earth from the space station, but the circle of transmat refractors has been broken. The Doctor needs to fix it with his sonic screwdriver."

"This is crap, isn't it?" I said.

I felt her bridle. "I love this show."

"That's because you're a nerd," I told her.

"Am I now?" she said, with a little moan.

"You're a geek and a dork, like your boyfriend."

"You have no respect for the things we like, do you?"

"Not at all. The only thing I like about you is you're so hot for my cock."

She hopped up and I gasped at the sudden absence of pussy around my cock. She went into Peter's room and came back with a comic book. "Peter and I love this," she said. "It's one of our favorites. I want to know what you think of it."

I wasn't in a place to get some reading done, but I knew that wasn't what she wanted, either. I flipped through the comic book, pretending to look at it. "This is shit," I pronounced. I made like I was going to rip it up.

"Please don't," she said, in a voice suggesting she both did and didn't want me to. I tore it in half then into quarters and threw it on the floor.

She gave me a look full of dark desire. "You bastard," she said in a low growl I'd never heard from her before. I'd have been happy if she'd sat on my dick again, but she bent over the couch, bracing herself on the armrest. "Fuck me hard," she said. "Show me how much you respect me."

I stood behind her, grabbed hold of her skinny hips, and drove my cock into her. I'd never felt her cunt so wet. If I'd been in any other position, it would have been hard not to slip out of her. I wanted to fuck her selfishly, without letting her have an orgasm, but she was too excited. She started cumming almost as soon as I was inside her. I let her cum on my cock, then thrust into her for a few more minutes. I was fucking her bareback, so couldn't cum inside her. I pulled out of her. I'd enjoyed cumming in her mouth before and thought about doing it again. In the end, I decided I had the perfect target in front of me. I tugged my cock twice and jetted my sperm over the round cheeks of her ass.

I wiped my dick on the tail of Peter's shirt. Would there be any of his clothes I *hadn't* seeded by the time we stopped doing this? Sophie and I didn't say another word to each other. She straightened up and sat down without even bothering to clean herself. She carried on watching her program. I went into my room feeling more relaxed and I did actually do a bit of work.

PETER

I'D LEARNED TO RECOGNIZE WHEN MARK was beginning his final approach and preparing for orgasm. After he'd made Sophie cum— or denied her, whatever he decided to do—he stopped touching or kissing her. He locked in to one position and looked at her intensely, almost angrily. The speed of his thrusts increased. Although this was supposed to be his time, Sophie told me she loved this bit. His cock pistoned in and out of her relentlessly with no changes in speed or pressure. It often brought her to another orgasm, but she did her best to hide this one as it wasn't the objective then. He never said anything during this part. He didn't call her names or remind her what she was doing. Often he knew exactly where he wanted to cum and would not be denied but, sometimes, before ejaculating, he asked her, "Where do you want it?"

She had three stock replies. The first was, "Anywhere you want." She didn't use this so much as she'd picked up he only asked this question when he wanted her to choose. I guess it was like him wanting her to beg him. There was something humiliating about a woman indicating a part of her body and asking a man to soil it with his seed. Her second answer was, "Belly." It turned her on to have a bellybutton full of cum. She always gazed at the cum excitedly and dipped the tip of her finger into it. She also liked me to lap it out of her bellybutton after Mark had gone.

This time, however, they were back in my bed and she said, "Tits." He nodded in approval. It was one of his favorites. He deliberately pulled out of her so suddenly she gasped. He knelt up and moved his way up the bed on his knees until he was by her chest. She took his cock in her left hand. Her rhythm isn't so good with that hand, but he was so close, it didn't matter. Two tugs and he was shooting all over my girlfriend's tits. I was always amazed by how much came out. I was lucky if I created a little pool in her cleavage. He covered her tits with thick ropes of the stuff. After he'd finished, he lay on the bed and spent a moment recovering his strength. He sat up and said, "I'd better leave you to . . . whatever it is you do at these moments."

Sophie put her hand on his arm. "Mark, could you stay?"

He shrugged. "I can stay a few minutes."

"I meant all night."

I did not like this idea at all. Sophie and I had our couple time after Mark had left. It was when we talked about what had happened. It made me feel like she had fucked Mark for no other reason but to turn me on. It was also the moment when I got to cum. It was the aftercare service I needed following the intensity of watching my girlfriend with another man. It seemed Mark didn't like the idea either. "I'm not sure I want to sleep in Peter's bed," he said.

"Please," said Sophie. There is something so painful but powerfully erotic about hearing your woman say 'please' to another man, especially if she's naked at the time.

An evil look crept into Mark's face. "How much is it worth?"

"What?" I demanded.

Sophie looked at me, calmly. "Pay him." I stared at her, open-mouthed. I couldn't believe she was seriously asking me to pay another man to sleep in my bed. Sitting up, she leaned toward me with her breasts fully visible. She squeezed my cock through my trousers and smiled as she felt it was rock hard. This was becoming her riposte every time I voiced any sort of protest. "You can't pretend you're not interested."

I wanted to scream the whole idea was ridiculous and who in their right mind would ever do something like that. All I said was, "How much?"

Mark looked so smug, I wanted to punch him, but I knew that wouldn't end well for me. "I'll take what you've got," he said. The blood was roaring in my ears as I took my wallet out of my jacket pocket and handed him all the cash inside it. I had the feeling we were crossing a line. Sophie took my wallet from me and checked I'd given him everything. She found a couple of coins in a zipped compartment and gave those to him. Once she was sure my wallet was empty, she tossed it back to me. He lay back on the bed. "I guess I'm sleeping here tonight," he said.

"I'm in your bed then," I said, resignedly.

He looked up sharply. "No one sleeps in my bed except for me and hot girls."

"Where do I sleep then?" I wanted to know.

"On the couch," said Sophie.

"I'll be cold and uncomfortable," I whined.

"Cold and uncomfortable," she repeated, a slow smile spreading across her face. A strange thrill ran through me. It was the first time that evening I felt like *I* was the source of Sophie's excitement.

I went out of my room, closing the door on Mark in my bed with my girlfriend. In the bathroom, I brushed my teeth and washed my face. Only when I got to the couch did I remember I'd left my pajamas in my room. I felt I'd been banished until morning. Lying down in my clothes added to my discomfort. Whichever way I turned, there was always a crease or a seam digging in to some part of me. I was angry. What gave them the right to kick me out of my own room? Nevertheless, I was surprised at my level of arousal. Here I was, sleeping on the couch because it was what my girlfriend and her lover wanted. It was unfair, but I was starting to realize unfairness was arousing. After all, it was unfair Sophie could see other men while I couldn't see other women. It was unfair that I, a poor student, paid for lingerie my girlfriend wore to attract another man. I was being exploited, treated badly like I was less important than Sophie and Mark. A masochistic part of me found this exciting. I felt like I was being punished, but for what? I hadn't done anything wrong. It's not like I'd tried to do stop them doing what they wanted to do. I was being punished simply for being me, the cuckold, bottom of the heap in this unequal relationship. It turned me on.

With all the lights in the pad turned off, I lay on the couch, straining my ears to hear what was happening in my bedroom. I heard their voices but didn't make out any words. It could have been dirty talk or a discussion of the weather. The bed wasn't creaking and Sophie wasn't moaning, so I guessed they weren't having sex. After a while, the talking stopped to be replaced by the low purr of Sophie snoring. It was a sound I liked to hear next to me because it reminded me I was in bed with a woman. I didn't know how Mark would react to it. He might find it annoying and go back to his own bed, leaving me free to join my girlfriend. I wasn't sure if I wanted that to happen or not.

There was no movement out of my room, so Mark either lived with the sound or went to sleep. I didn't know what to do. The emotions of anger and arousal churning inside me made sleep unlikely. I could have dampened some of my emotions by jerking off, but I decided the effects would only be negative. I wouldn't be excited anymore but I'd still be aggrieved. That wouldn't make it any easier to sleep. I tried thinking about other things. Maybe if I ran some favorite movies in my head from beginning to end, it would get me through the night. It's hard to focus on anything else when your girlfriend is with another man a few yards from where you're lying. I resigned myself to a long night of staring into the darkness.

The next thing I knew, sunlight was coming through the window and I was aware of someone moving through the den. The soft pad of small bare feet told me it was Sophie. I kept my eyes closed until her hair brushed against my face as she kissed me. "How was your night, babe?" she asked.

Remembering how much the words had turned her on the night before, I looked her in the eye and intoned, "Cold and uncomfortable."

I heard that little moan again. "I was warm and comfortable in bed."

"My bed," I reminded her.

"In your bed," she agreed. "In Mark's arms. He's got big, strong arms. I felt so safe as he held me."

This sounded more like love than sex. I wasn't comfortable with going down that road just yet so I changed the subject slightly. "Did you . . . do anything else last night?"

Sophie sat on the couch, undid my jeans, and put her hand in to tease the tip of my cock between her forefinger and thumb. "Well . . . I woke up at about two. Mark was spooning me and his crotch was up against my naked butt." I took a moment to picture this. She continued, "He had this enormous erection. I like to think it was because I was in bed with him, but he might have been dreaming about someone else. It seemed a shame to waste a good, hard cock, so I squirmed down the bed until my head was level with his crotch. I put his cock into my mouth. It felt like such a quiet moment in the peace of the night that I didn't suck it. I licked it and kind of gave it a tongue bath. It was all so gentle. I'm not sure he even woke up completely. At one point, he put his hand on my head. He also said, "Feels good," but he didn't say my name or anything, so I've no idea if he knew it was me. Anyway, my gentle ministrations worked. I made him cum, but it was different from normal. It wasn't his usual great long spurts. It was more of a slow ooze into my mouth."

I was almost afraid to ask the next question. "What did you do with it?"

She bit her lip and gave me a roguish look. "I swallowed if of course. It's what I do when Mark comes in my mouth."

"It wasn't to turn him on if he was barely conscious."

"It was mainly for me," she said. "Plus I knew I'd be telling you about it."

"You are so slutty, Sophie."

"You thought you were getting a sweet, innocent girlfriend. Instead, you got a dirty whore. You love it, don't you?"

"Yes, I do."

"Do you want to cum, Peter?" she asked me.

"I need to," I replied.

"Where do you want to cum? In my mouth? All over my face and hair? Do you want to cover my tits? Or maybe you want me to catch it in my hand and rub it all over myself. Would you like that?"

I could barely breathe. "Yes," I said with difficulty, "I . . . would like that very much."

Standing up, she said, "Sorry, Peter. I'd better get back and see if Mark's awake yet."

She went into my bedroom, closing the door behind her. I slumped across the couch, devastated, but walking away was the sexiest thing she could have done.

Eighteen

PETER

Teasing and denial became an important part of my time with Sophie. Two weeks after my first night on the couch, Sophie came round to the pad. I was glad Mark was off at practice as it meant I could have an evening alone with my girlfriend. I felt it was what I needed. After we'd eaten dinner and I'd kept my promise to keep her always supplied with tea, we wordlessly agreed it was time to take things into my bedroom.

Sophie took off all her clothes. It was a while since I'd experienced her body without seeing it through Mark's eyes. This time, she undressed for no other reason than to turn *me* on. No one was interested in watching me do a slow and sensuous striptease, so I pulled off my shirt, pants, and underwear with a minimum of fuss, remembering of course to remove my socks. She lay on the bed and beckoned me to join her. I instinctively tried to touch her but she gently pushed my hand away. "No hands. Use your lips. Kiss me."

I was happy to do this. We craned our necks forward like a couple of turtles and kissed. Our kisses had been chaste of late, and I was happy and excited when she opened her mouth wide and flicked the tip of her tongue against mine. If I'd stayed quiet and let things happen, we'd have had sex. If there's one thing I'm no good at, it's staying quiet. "Sophie, can I ask you something?"

With her trademark eye roll, she said, "By any chance, is it something about Mark, or infidelity, or cuckoldry, or . . .."

"Right first time. It's about Mark."

She sighed but said, "Go on."

"What does he call it?"

"Call what?" she asked, even though she had a good idea what I was talking about.

"You know, the thing he's got between his legs, the one that fills you?"

"I'm not sure," she said, frowning. Giving me a playful look, she added, "He doesn't speak as much as you do. He lets his cock do the talking." She realized she'd unwittingly answered my question. "Yes, I'm pretty sure he calls it his cock."

I put Sophie's hand on my penis and said, "That's mine."

"Evidently," she said, wondering what I was getting at.

"That's as big as it gets. It doesn't compare with Mark's, does it?"

"No," she admitted.

"We've been calling it my cock, but it needs another name."

"It's very different from the other cock in our lives, so yes it does. What did you have in mind?"

"We should call it my willy. It's what little boys call their penises."

"You've only got a little boy's penis."

"Exactly."

She laughed. "Works for me. I notice your willy is erect," she told me, unnecessarily, as I was well aware of the fact. "It means your body is ready for sex." I knew that too but had no objection to her talking about it. She put her hand between her legs and touched herself. "You know what, Peter? My pussy is wet." She moved her hand up and waved her finger under my nose. "Do I smell good?"

"You smell gorgeous," I said, hoarsely. For once, her juices were untainted by Mark's cum.

"My body is also preparing for sex." We were both well enough prepared and ready to get started. "What do you want to do now?" she asked with a teasing smile.

"I want to fuck you."

"Mark's the one who fucks me these days."

"I want to make love to you then."

"That's nice, but do you know what I want to do?"

"What?"

"Sleep. It's been a long day." Kissing me lightly on the nose, she said, "Good night."

I was surprised at the next words that came out of my mouth. "Teasing bitch!" I regretted it as soon as I said it and wanted to retract it.

Her face was thoughtful rather than offended. Slowly, her mouth twisted into a smile. "Yes, I am a teasing bitch and I like it." She looked me in the eye and added, "So do you." She rolled onto her side with her back to me. "You face the other way," she told me. "No touching in the night. And, Peter," she added, warningly, "that means no touching me and no touching yourself."

The no masturbation clause had been implied before. This was the first time it had been made explicit. She was soon asleep. I was jealous of her because I didn't think I'd get any sleep. With Sophie out for the night, there was nothing to stop me giving myself a little relief. I didn't, though, as it wouldn't have been playing the game.

NINETEEN

SOPHIE

EVERY TIME I TOOK OFF MY clothes and climbed into bed next to Peter, I had a feeling of safety, knowing exactly what was going to happen. Peter had found a way of giving me pleasure and he wasn't going to mess with a formula that worked. He gazed at me like he'd never seen me before and said, "You're beautiful." I like being told I'm beautiful, but I sometimes wished he'd change the record. If you're told the same thing in the same tone of voice at the same time often enough, it stops meaning anything. He then kissed me. Don't get me wrong, I like kissing, but I could almost hear him counting to a thousand in his head so he knew he'd been doing it long enough. Then he moved down my body. One thing I genuinely loved about Peter was that he found every part of me sexy. Like everyone, I'm often insecure about my body. I come home after a long day and I'm appalled by the state of my body, especially my armpits and feet. They're like quicksand patches on building land—not only undesirable in themselves but devaluing everything around them. Peter made me feel good about these parts again, even if his way of doing it was a bit odd. He kissed and licked my armpits, then held his face in front of mine to make sure I could see his expression—like he was enjoying a fine wine. Then he moved to my feet, sucking each toe in turn, before making exaggerated yummy noises as he kissed and licked the soles. He was never going to make me cum by stimulating my armpits or feet, so there was no natural endpoint. He kept going until he'd made his point that every little part of me was deeply erotic to him. When he finally finished, he did something adorably caring and responsible. He hopped off the bed, went to his basin, and gargled with antiseptic mouth-wash to kill any foot germs before he went down on me. As soon as his head was lodged between my thighs, I made myself comfortable, knowing we were going to be there for a while. Peter had the idea that if he made me cum with his tongue, I'd be satisfied and couldn't complain if he spent only a few minutes inside me. I understood his thinking, but I wished he'd mix it up a bit. As our relationship progressed, he got a lot better at hitting the right spot with his tongue. At the start, I had to give instructions like I was talking down a plane, "A bit to the left. Raise the nose a little. Don't go in too fast. Straighten up. Now bring her home." After a couple of months, he sometimes managed it without any input from me at all. I could simply lie back and let it happen. Very pleasant it was too.

After I'd cum, Peter asked me if I wanted another one. Unless we were playing the denial game, I smiled and said, "No, it's your turn."

He carefully lay on top of me. I put my hand around the base of his cock, or his willy as we'd agreed to call it. I put it in my pussy. Peter stayed as still as possible when he was inside me, afraid that any movement would make him cum too quickly. That's when he told me, "Oh, Sophie, you are so beautiful. I'm in love with your body. It looks so good, tastes so good, feels so good. I'm so lucky to be with you."

All very nice but I found myself fighting the urge to say, "It's a naked female body, get over it."

Only then did he move inside me, as tentatively as if he were polishing a priceless antique vase. At the same time he kissed my lips and neck, as if hoping the icing would make up for a bland cake. It was nice to feel close to my boyfriend and to know how much he loved me. Physically, though, it wasn't exactly mind blowing. I knew I could end it any time I wanted. All I had to do was moan and say, "Oh, Mark . . . sorry, Peter." This always made Peter cum immediately. However much he clenched his body and tried to do math problems in his head, he couldn't stop the inevitable. He squirted his little bit of watery semen either into the condom or over my breasts.

Afterwards, we lay together. We'd gotten into the habit of lying with his head on my chest rather than the more traditional other way round. I suppose it gave him more up close and personal time with my boobs. He had his eyes closed, but I was staring at the ceiling. I had just had sex. I had cum. Why wasn't that enough for me? Why did I still want more? I thought about riding it out. Peter had math problems. I had certain politicians I didn't like. If I focused hard enough on them, I hoped my ardor would fade. It was no good: I had an itch which needed to be scratched.

Peter's breathing deepened and I dared to hope he'd fallen asleep. I started the sideways horizontal shuffle of trying to get out from under him without waking him up. "What are you doing?" he asked, dashing my hopes.

"I'm going next door for a minute."

"Why do you have to do that?" he whined. "We made love."

Kissing his forehead, I said, "Yes, we did, and it was great. Now I need to be fucked."

"Give me a minute and I'll fuck you."

"You can do that later when you've got your strength back. For now, try to get some rest." I sat up in bed, put my hand under the quilt, and gave Peter's willy a squeeze—partly to give him a thrill, partly to check he was all right with what I was doing. He was rock hard, which I took as a sign of approval.

I didn't bother putting on any clothes. I went to the door, wiggling my ass, because I knew Peter was watching me go. I walked the three steps between doors. At Mark's door, I stopped and listened. I was pretty sure he was alone. The walls were thin and I could hear what was going on in Mark's room. I hadn't heard any voices or sex noises. I knocked on the door and pushed it open. "Mark?" I said, softly.

"Who is it?" he asked.

This was him being annoying. He knew perfectly well who it was. "It's Sophie," I said, playing along.

I went in, closing the door behind me. I made my way to his bed in darkness. It felt deliciously naughty to slide between the sheets of my second man that evening. "Was it my imagination," he began, "or did I hear you and Peter doing whatever it is you do a bit earlier?"

"Yes, but he didn't satisfy me." I felt bad, talking about my boyfriend like this, but Mark liked to hear it.

He took my hand and placed it on his cock. I had another delicious moment as I realized this was the second cock I'd touched in less than a minute. I felt both guilty and proud of myself at the same time. "He doesn't have a cock like this," said Mark.

"No, he doesn't," I agreed.

"He doesn't fuck you like I do."

My heart beat faster and my body squirmed closer to his. "How do you fuck me, Mark?"

"Hard and fast," he told me. "I fuck you like the whore you are."

"Fuck me now," I said. "Fuck your little whore."

He locked his lips to mine. My jaw cracked as I opened my mouth as wide as possible to accommodate Mark's tongue. Peter's tongue always felt like a lizard's—tentatively scoping out the area. Mark's was like a wrecking ball—nothing was going to get in its way. His tongue filled my mouth, violating it, preparing me for the next thing that would violate me. As we kissed, he squeezed my tits hard. I wanted him to fuck me but his hands were on my shoulders, pushing me down until my head was level with his crotch. I hardly ever performed oral on Peter. The poor guy was so paranoid about his willy he didn't want to inflict it on anyone's mouth. Mark had no such concerns. He considered it a privilege for any woman to have his cock in her mouth. I wrapped my hand around the base of his cock. That still left plenty free to go into my mouth. I rubbed my tongue around his cock head, probing his cum hole with the tip. Keeping the flat of my tongue against the underside of his cock, I moved my head back and forth. I was glad when he tapped my head and told me to come back up. My mouth was not the place I wanted his cock. I didn't have to wait long to get what I did want. He rolled me gently onto my back. I didn't have to guide him in. His cock slid into me first time. I gasped at the sudden feeling of fullness. I should have been used to Mark's cock by then, but there was always a moment of wonder when he entered me. As he thrust his dick into me, he murmured in my ear, "Your boyfriend's next door."

"He's not the one I want right now," I replied.

"You dirty cheating bitch," he said. "You are such a slut for my cock, Sophie."

Now, I know I should disapprove of guys talking to me like that and ordinarily, I do. If someone in the street shouted anything like that at me, I would report them. Being massively turned on is like being drunk. Bad things can seem good. The more he called me bad names, the more excited I got. As he whispered, "Cheap little cunt," in my ear, I groaned and came on his cock. He gave a little laugh of triumph, then kept on thrusting. "You can have another one if you like."

I was in awe of his self-control. I vowed one day to test Mark to the limit and see how many times he could make me cum. For now, though, I was keen to get back to Peter. Yes, that was an important part of it for me. "No, it's your turn now," I told Mark.

"Where do you want it?"

"How about over my tits?"

"Your little slutty tits?"

He knelt up on the bed beside me. "You hate my tits, don't you?" I asked, pushing them together to make a better target.

"Yes, I do," he said, pulling on his cock. "I like big, lush tits, not skanky little gnat bites like yours."

"Show me how much you hate them," I said. He did, by cumming over them in two long stripes.

He wiped his cock clean on my belly and said, "Go back to Peter." It was part of our sexual MO. He used me and then tossed me out straight after.

"Don't you want me to stay a while?" I asked, playing along.

"Why?" he responded. "I got what I wanted."

If he didn't want me, there was someone who did. I knew Peter would have the light on when I went back into his room. He liked to see the traces Mark left on my body. As I got back into bed with my boyfriend, he said, "You went away smelling of me and came back smelling of him."

"What can you smell?" I asked him.

"His cologne first of all. That's strong stuff he wears."

"It turns me on. It's manly."

"Maybe I should get some."

"I'm not sure it would suit you, babe." I moved my face toward Peter's like I was going to kiss him. Instead, I held the tip of his nose lightly between my teeth. Breathing straight into his nostrils, I asked, "What can you smell there?"

Peter was breathless with lust as he replied, "I smell cock."

"It's not yours, is it?"

"No."

"How do you know it's not yours?"

"You never suck my willy."

"No, I don't. That's because your willy's too small, it's ugly, and it tastes like last week's fish. Mark's is big and beautiful and tastes so good." Peter was whimpering like a hungry puppy. There was a danger he'd cum from me insulting his willy. While that would have been entertaining, there was a job I wanted him to do first. I moved six inches away from him, put my left hand behind his head, and pulled it to my bosom. "What do you smell there, Peter?"

"Your tits smell of cum."

"Yes, they do. Mark decided my cunt wasn't worth cumming in, so he shot his load all over the tits you love so much." The sound coming out of Peter was low, guttural, primal. "You're not going to let me go to sleep with dirty tits, are you?"

He looked scared and horribly fascinated in equal measure. "You don't want me to . . .?"

"Yes, I do. You've already licked a bit of Mark's cum off my chin, so this is a small step."

His face showed an internal struggle. It was not a small step for him. I later learned it's something every cuckold goes through. He watches another man fuck his wife or girlfriend and finds himself admiring a big, beautiful cock. This is unsettling for a straight guy. Then comes the suggestion that he clean his woman following her act of infidelity. Some guys taste their own cum out of curiosity but, again, a heterosexual male doesn't have much reason to taste another man's seed so his brain reels at the realization of what he's doing. The ultimate is if he finds himself sucking the bull's cock or even being fucked up the ass. The dilemma for the cuckold is deciding how far along that road he wants to go. When he watches his woman with her stud, he can kid himself he's only looking at her. If he licks cum out of her pussy, he justifies it by saying she's just unusually wet. He can't tell himself he's still a hundred per cent straight if he has a cock in his mouth or his ass.

I guess Peter decided that licking a pair of tits was still a heterosexual act, no matter what sort of dressing was on them. He lapped at them, licking up Mark's cum. I put my arms around his head, cradling him. It was a dark and perverted version of breast feeding. The eroticism of it wasn't lost on Peter. Before even one breast was clean, I felt something warm and wet on my thigh. He assumed that, now he'd cum, the session was over and went for a post-coital cuddle. "Finish the job, Peter," I said, sternly. I know this is wrong, but I enjoyed him licking it more after he'd cum. I knew it was giving him no pleasure at all, and that turned me on. When both my tits were clean, I reminded him, "I still have cum on me, Peter."

"I can't!"

"You can and you will!"

It was his second cum of the evening so there was only a small patch on my thigh. One upward motion of his tongue was enough to get rid of it. After that, I finally held him in my arms. He was shaking uncontrollably and I was afraid I'd gone too far. After five minutes, he looked up into my face and said, "I can't wait to do that again."

TWENTY

SOPHIE

YOU KNOW THERE ARE MORNINGS WHERE you wake up and decide you want to do something? You're not always sure why. It might be something minor like deciding to have waffles for breakfast or buy a new pen. It could be a turning point in your life like choosing to marry one person over another or to train as a lawyer rather than a doctor. One morning, I woke up with a strong conviction about something I wanted to do. I wasn't sure how to make it happen, but I knew I wouldn't tell Peter about it until it was too late for him to stop it.

It was one of those things that's hard to work into conversation, so I let my body do most of the talking. Mark was out when I arrived at the pad. After I'd left my bag in the corner of the room, Peter and I sat around in the den talking and drinking tea. As casually as I could, I asked Peter, "Do you know when Mark's coming back?"

Peter shrugged. "He didn't say."

"Babe, could you text him and ask?"

"Why, because I'm missing him so much?"

"You can tell him how much *I'm* missing him."

His breathing quickened at this little cuckold humiliation. He pressed some buttons on his phone and said, "That's sent." Thirty seconds later, his phone bleeped and he said, "Mark's going to be here in ten minutes." I stood up and took off my jeans. Underneath, I was wearing a black, lacy thong, the back of which barely covered the crack of my ass. "What are you doing?" asked Peter.

I put a teasing finger to my lips so he'd stop talking. He sat in the chair and waited to see what would happen. When I heard Mark's key in the lock, I lay face down on the couch and directed my best sultry look at the door. As he came in, he called out, "How's it . . .?" He trailed off as he saw the scene in front of him. "Good to be greeted by a big smile," he said. I wasn't smiling but then he wasn't talking about my face. He perched on the edge of the couch and put his hand on my butt. I always liked Mark's touch. Peter was gentle to the point of being tentative and it tickled a little. Mark was firm and confident.

"Peter . . . sometimes inserts a finger," I pointed out, casually.

"We've established many times that Peter is a pervert," replied Mark.

"True. It feels nice, though."

"I don't go around fingering girls' butts."

My heart was beating fast as I said, "Well . . . it wouldn't neces-sarily . . . have to be . . . a finger."

Peter would have spent twenty minutes checking that I really meant what he thought I meant. Mark understood immediately. "No, it wouldn't, but if you want it to happen, Sophie, I have to hear you say it properly."

I was surprised I didn't feel nervous as I said, "Mark, would you fuck me up my ass?"

Peter had been slower on the uptake. Only now did he gasp. "Sophie! You said you never wanted to do that."

"Maybe I've changed my mind," I said.

"Or maybe she didn't want to do it *with you*," suggested Mark.

"Can you help me get ready, Peter?" I asked.

"We don't have anything we can use, so let's leave it until we're better prepared."

"Look in my bag," I said. He went to the bag I'd dumped in the corner of the room and looked inside. I'd brought a small tub of unscented moisturizer cream. Mark stood up so Peter could take his place on the couch. I raised my crotch off the bed as Peter eased down my thong and took it off. He opened the tub. "Use lots," I said. "Don't worry about wasting it. You can always buy me some more later."

Peter used the finger and thumb of his left hand in a reverse pincer to open me up. "Are you sure?" he said.

There was genuine concern in his voice, so I asked, "What's the matter?"

"Your asshole looks like the eye of a needle. I'm not sure I can get my finger in there. No way can it take Mark's cock."

"It'll be fine. Just do it, please, Peter." I shivered as the cold cream touched my asshole for the first time. Peter's finger worked its way inside me.

"Your asshole's surprisingly elastic," said Peter.

"Why, thank you," I replied. "You say the nicest things."

"I've got two fingers inside you now," he said.

It felt good, but I wanted something else in there. "Thank you, Peter, that's enough."

Peter stood up and moved aside. Mark maneuvered his body onto mine. I *was* a little bit scared as he positioned the head of his cock between my buttocks. It felt like a fist. It entered me more easily than I'd expected. Peter had done a good job of lubing me up. There was pain, especially as Mark penetrated me. My rectum was not used to things moving in that direction. There was also a tingle. Nerve endings were being stimulated in unfamiliar ways. Most of all, there was a feeling of daring naughtiness. I've heard of porn stars who refuse to do this. Here was I, little Sophie, going where some porn stars feared to tread. Mark was a lot more gentle than normal. He knew my pussy could take the full force of his thrusts. My delicate asshole was not so resilient. Waves of mixed pain and pleasure were breaking over me, but I knew I wasn't going to cum. He picked up on this and didn't try to make it happen. He increased the speed of his thrusts slightly. It wasn't too long before I felt something wet and warm flooding into a place where it didn't belong. Mark pulled out, wiped his cock on my right buttock, and walked out of the pad without another word. It might have been my imagination but the look on his face had a hint of guilt in it.

It would have been fun to make Peter clean me with his tongue but I hadn't checked how toxic the moisturizer cream was. We'd need to get hold of some edible lube if we were going to make a habit of this. Peter used a tissue to clean my ass, which I guess was humiliating enough for him. Then we lay together on the couch. Even though Peter's arms were around me, Mark was one in my head. I felt he'd known me more intimately than anyone had before. I felt very close to him at that moment.

MARK

I ALWAYS MAKE IT CLEAR WHEN I start fucking a woman that I'm not offering anything more than a short break from her humdrum life. While her boring husband is off at his sensible job and she takes a break from screaming at the kids, she can sit back and smile as she remembers her times with me. I'm not going to be her boyfriend and I'm certainly never going to be that boring husband of hers. Despite this, there's always a girl who reckons that, because she's so fabulous, she'll make me change my entire lifestyle and settle down with her. This was Sophie's thinking when she offered me her ass. She naïvely hoped this would make me stay because I couldn't turn my back on a woman who did something so kinky.

I felt sorry for Peter and Sophie. Letting another man into their relationship was life-changing for them. They couldn't believe they had taken such a step. For me, Sophie was just another conquest. I enjoyed exploring her body and fucking her was fun, but she was like any other woman in that there were limits to what she had to offer. I'd put my cock in her mouth, between her tits, in her cunt, and up her ass. I'd made her jerk me off and smear my cum all over her face and tits. She didn't have much experience so didn't have a range of kinky ideas to keep me interested. What did she have left to give me? The answer was nothing.

The thing that had kept me interested in Sophie longer than in most women was that she was my roommate's girlfriend. Everyday interactions with Peter had a subtext to them. "Morning, Peter, did you sleep well? (I've seen your girlfriend naked.) Hey, Peter, how was your day? (Your girlfriend sat on my dick last night and I made her cum like a bitch.)"

As sad I was for Sophie, I felt worse for Peter, as he was my friend. For a moment, it made me think I should keep friendship separate from my sex life. I quickly dismissed the idea. I knew if I met a guy who had a hot wife or girlfriend, I wouldn't be able to resist however much I liked him. Peter probably thought we were in a throuple, or some new age nonsense like that. Maybe he had a fantasy of marrying Sophie and me sharing his wife's bed while he slept on the floor and watched me fucking her when I gave him permission. I could see that would be fun to do once, but it would soon get boring.

Over the last few days, I'd been looking at Sophie and Peter, with a growing feeling it was time to move on. It's not that they had changed. It's simply that I'd done everything I wanted to do in this scenario. It's never an easy conversation to have. Despite what you might think, I'm not a complete bastard. I do what I do and know some feelings are going to be trampled along the way, but I try to minimize the damage if I can.

Opening the door to the pad, I found Sophie and Peter in the den. I felt a pang as I looked at Sophie. They had obviously been on one of their shopping trips. She was wearing scarlet panties with a crisscross pattern going up her belly and chest. The pattern was repeated in the bra, with the cross centers concealing Sophie's nipples. She gave me her best seductive look as I came in. "Hi, Mark," she said.

"Hello," I replied.

"Like what you see?"

"It's nice."

She picked up on my muted responses. "What's wrong?"

"Sophie," I began, "I've enjoyed getting to know you."

"Is that what you call it?" she muttered.

"We've had some good times, but it's the end of the line."

Her face fell. "I've given you everything."

"I appreciate that."

"Things I've never even done with Peter ... or anyone."

"Most women I know offer me all three holes to play with. That was a much bigger deal for you than it was for me."

I couldn't blame her for the look of pure fury she gave me. I stayed on alert in case she flew at me. The anger in her eyes soon faded to be replaced by sadness. "So I'm wearing this for nothing then?"

"We can have a farewell fuck, if you like," I suggested.

Sophie would have been well within her rights to respond with an angry, "Fuck you!" rather than a sensual, "Fuck me." To be honest, I'd have respected her if she'd said that. Her mouth tightened into a determined, thin line as she said, "Okay, come on." She led the way into Peter's room. I was pleased about this. The final fuck is often a good one.

She sat on Peter's bed, pulled me toward her, and aggressively yanked down my pants and shorts. Grabbing the base of my cock, she put her lips around it and sucked it hard. After a few minutes, she paused to look up at me and asked, "Do you want me to keep going, so you can cum in my mouth? Would you prefer to stick your big, hard cock in my warm, wet cunt or maybe up my tight, little asshole?"

It's something many a girl has done when she's been told it's the last time with me. She goes out of her way to show how filthy she is. I'm supposed to get the fear I'll never find anyone so dirty again and change my mind about dumping her. It's never worked yet, but it does make for a good farewell fuck. I decided to keep it traditional. I laid her on the bed. I didn't kiss her because I wanted to avoid too much intimacy, but I did want to see her tits one last time. I pushed up her bra and her nipples popped out. I knew they'd spent a lot of money on this lingerie so I grabbed the gusset of her panties in my fist. I gave a quick tug. There was a sound of seams ripping. Sophie's nicely shaven cunt was on display with the ruined waistband of her panties still round her middle. Peter groaned with despair and his girlfriend moaned with outraged desire. It was possibly the last time that ever happened to her, I don't know. Peter would never do that. He might not even have the strength to ensure a clean rip. I kissed her pussy one last time to say goodbye. I lay on top of her and inserted my cock. I wanted to make her final memories of me good ones. I kept a steady rhythm inside her until her body bucked and she came. Then I simply kept on going until she came again. As her orgasm subsided, she started to cry. This isn't uncommon. It's like tears on the flight home after a great holiday. Once the excitement's over, it's replaced with sadness at going back to humdrum life. If Sophie had asked me to stop, I would have, but she didn't. I've no objection to fucking a weeping woman. The worlds of sex, love, and desire in which I move are ones that encourage strong emotions. I kept fucking her for a while before pulling out and moving up her body. I took her right hand and put it on my cock. She knew what I wanted and pulled my cock hard while aiming the tip at her tits. I came over them. I knew exactly what she was going to do next. She got between my legs and licked my softening cock clean. The message was clear. You'll never find another bitch so perverted that she'll suck you after you've cum. She was still crying, her tears falling on my pubes and my balls.

After she'd finished, I pulled my pants up and went out, leaving Peter and Sophie to it.

PETER

I SAT WITH MY BACK AGAINST THE headboard of my bed. Sophie sobbed on my chest, soaking my shirt in her tears. "I can't … believe … he left me," she said, trying to catch her breath. It sounded like she was crying to her best friend. I was glad that was me. It also sounded like she was crying about her boyfriend, but that was me too. It was a strange situation to be in, comforting my own girlfriend over the loss of her man.

She stayed in my bed for the next couple of days. Neither of us went to any lectures. I held her, brought her food, read to her, and played her music. She was also in the unusual position of having her boyfriend still with her to comfort her after the break up.

TWENTY-ONE

PETER

EVEN FOR SOMEONE AS BRAZEN AS Mark, it would have been awkward to keep sharing a room with me after everything that had happened. He said he was going to bunk down with one of his soccer playing friends for a few days to give Sophie and me some space. One morning when I came back to the pad from a lecture, I found all Mark's stuff had gone. I felt sad. I wasn't sure I could still call it the pad, as that was the name Mark and I had given to *our* place. I missed his TV and fridge. I hated him for the way he'd treated Sophie at the end, but I was grateful to him for being a friend. I could also see possibilities here. Mark had left his key on the coffee table. I knew whose pocket that was going into.

Sophie never officially moved in. She still had her own room in the other building, but spent more time at the pad. She could sleep in my bed if she wanted to be jammed up against another human being all night or in Mark's old bed when she needed some space. It was also a place that had good memories for her.

I was sitting on the couch in the den. With the TV gone, I was forced to read a book. I loved hearing a key in the lock and knowing it was Sophie. She walked in and sat in the chair. "How was your day?" she asked, in a voice that told me she was just being polite. She didn't really want to know.

"Fine," I said. "Yours?"

"Also fine." The formalities required by polite society had been completed. There was a moment's silence. "Hug me," she said, flatly. I didn't know what to make of the way she said it, but I knelt by her chair and gathered her into my arms. "Do I smell of another man's cologne?" she asked.

This was a surprise. What had she been doing and why hadn't she talked to me about it first? I sniffed her all over. "No, you don't," I said, truthfully.

"What do I smell of?"

"Clean clothes and perfume. You smell lovely."

She sighed. "Lovely or boring? I can't believe I'll never come to you smelling of Mark again."

"You will never be boring to me."

This was her opportunity to tell me I'd never be boring to her, either. What she did say was genuinely hurtful. "I miss Mark."

Being a cuckold is often confusing. The pain of hearing that was immediately matched by excitement at my girlfriend's casual cruelty. I tried to hide my feelings with a bland comment. "We had some exciting times with him."

"I suppose it was always going to end like this. He'd move on, knowing you and I would be all right because we have each other."

I kissed her and said, "Yes, we do."

"It's something I've been meaning to talk to you about," continued Sophie. "We can't put the cork back in the bottle, Peter. If you stay with me, this is your life. I'll never be faithful to you. I'll expect your understanding and support with every new man who comes into our bed. There are times when it will annoy the hell out of you. We might be going to see a show or off on a trip and I'll turn around as we're heading out the door if there's the smallest possibility of getting some random guy's dick inside me. You'll have to chalk up the wasted time and money to part of your punishment for being a cuck. If we get married, I'll have another man's cum leaking out of me as I say my vows. If we have kids, you'll never know if they're yours or not. Either way, you'll have to look after them while I'm out getting fucked. I'll crawl back into our bed at two in the morning with a stranger's cologne on my body, his cock on my breath, and his cum all over my tits and in my hair. Is that what you want?"

I knew she was talking like this to excite me and I should simply have gone along with her fantasy vision of what our future would be. As it was, I gazed at my lovely girlfriend and said, "There was another way things could have ended with Mark."

She looked at me, intrigued. "How's that, babe?"

"He could have stolen you away from me."

We knew we were approaching a dark place and we both decided to go there. "Is that something you thought about?" she asked.

"Oh yes, I often lay in bed, looking at you, thinking how lucky I was to have you. I imagined what it would be like if you weren't there anymore. When you were off with Mark, I always worried this would be the time you didn't come back. After all, if you were having such a good time with him, why would you bother with me?"

Sophie gave me an evil little smile. "What did you do while you were having these thoughts, Peter?"

"I masturbated."

Nodding, she said, "You were in bed, enjoying the warmth of your girlfriend beside you. You wondered what it would be like if you were cold and all alone. The masochistic part of you liked that idea."

"I imagined you sitting me down and telling me it was over between us."

"You'd look at my body inside my clothes and know you'd never see me naked again."

"I'd give you one last hug, breathe in your scent, and know I'd never be that close to you again."

"Maybe I'd be like Mark and let you fuck me one last time, giving you a final taste of what you'd never get again. Would that be cruel enough for you?"

"Not as cruel as making me watch you with your new boyfriend. He has a lifetime of seeing and touching you ahead of him. The last time I ever see your body, you'll be using it to excite the man who's taking my place."

"You've thought a lot about this, haven't you, Peter?"

I decided to be honest with her, which is rarely a good idea when it comes to a man's musings about sex. "It's the culmination of the cuckold dream. I encourage you to have sex with another man. Then you come back to me and say, 'Oh babe, I've just had the best fuck of my life. He's so much better than you.' It's devastating for me as a man to know that, in this fundamental way, some other guy is better than me. I take huge comfort, though, in the fact that you've come back to me. I'm the one you want to be with after the excitement has gone. You want me to hold you and reassure you that you're still loved. But what's so great about me? What keeps you coming back? What if you found one person who could both love you like you want to be loved and fuck you like you need to be fucked? You wouldn't need me anymore, so you'd cut me out of the picture. You'd say goodbye and leave me alone and cold in an empty bed. I'd look at the place where you used to be and spend the night crying and masturbating, the twin activities of the cuckold. I'd be crying because I can't believe I was so stupid. I had this wonderful girlfriend. I loved her. She loved me. Why wasn't that enough? Why did I want to make some dumb cuckold fantasy into reality? What did I think was going to happen if I encouraged my girlfriend to have great sex with other guys? Of course she'd end up leaving me for one of them. I'd be masturbating to the thought of you in his bed. He gets to kiss you. He sees you naked every day. He fucks you every night before going to sleep and again when he wakes up. I'd give everything I own for one more time with you. He gets it for free any time he wants. It's not just the sex, but also the intimacy. He goes to sleep with his arm around you. Your feet are in his lap while you watch TV. He's the one who sits on the side of the bath and chats to you while you're naked surrounded by bubbles. I'm intensely jealous of him but I can't get mad at him because I'm the one who encouraged you to get with him. That's when I start crying again."

Sophie stood up and took off her clothes. She motioned me to do the same. As soon as I was naked, she lay on the couch and pulled me on top of her. She took hold of my willy and fed it into her pussy. "I know you love me, Peter," she said, "so I know it would break your heart if I ever left you."

Kissing her neck, I moved inside her. "Would that turn you on?" I asked. "Breaking my heart?"

She put her arms behind her head, showing me the armpits that suited Mark's tastes, not mine. "Yes, it would," she said. "I never thought any man would feel about me the way you do. That gives me power over you. Breaking your heart would be the ultimate exercise of that power."

"Could you do that to me?"

"It's not that I *could* do that to you. I *will* do that to you. We're going to find other guys for me to cuckold you with. You're going to love watching me flirting. Then the first kiss, the touching, the undressing, until he puts his dick up me and you see that, once again, I'm being the unfaithful girlfriend you know and love so much. There'll always be that worry eating away at you. Maybe this will be the guy I leave you for. I will do it, Peter. It might be next week or it might be twenty years from now, but I will leave you a broken man with your heart in pieces. Is that what you want?"

My heart was on top of hers. Both were thumping. I kissed her. The realization that every kiss might be the last made it extra passionate. "Yes, I want that very much."

"So do I," she said. "We have an exciting journey ahead of us, Peter. Now fuck me."

ABOUT THE AUTHOR

Rob's life changed one Saturday morning, when his girl-friend came home after spending the night at her friend's place. She climbed into bed next to him and said, "Rob, I've been a bad girl. I wasn't at Leanne's last night. I was with Nick. We had sex three times." Rob was deeply hurt, very angry, and massively turned on. He had never experienced such an intense cocktail of emotions before. This sent Rob down the rabbit hole, talking to cuckolds, hot wives, and Bulls about why people are attracted to this lifestyle and why it provokes such strong feelings. Rob is the author of the Cuckold Odyssey series: *Come Home With Us*; *I Can Do It Better*; *We Make Our Own Rules*; and *I'm The One You Need*. He has also written two stand-alone interracial cuckold books, *Black and Blue* and *Talking Bull*. Rob's books have been praised for being highly erotic but also a realistic insight into the highs and lows of cuckoldry. *A Cuckold Begins* is the first volume of Rob's new series. The follow-up *A Cuckold Breaks* is coming soon.

www.ingramcontent.com/pod-product-compliance
Lightning Source LLC
Chambersburg PA
CBHW011519100726
47899CB00010BD/3429